DADDY'S BEST FRIEND

K.C. CROWNE

Copyright © 2019 by K.C. Crowne

All rights reserved.

No part of this book may be reproduced in any form or by any electronic or mechanical means, including information storage and retrieval systems, without written permission from the author, except for the use of brief quotations in a book review.

❦ Created with Vellum

DESCRIPTION

**Matthew isn't just older...
He's my dad's best friend.
And my new hot boss.**

*I've always been a good girl.
Played by all the rules...
But, now that Matthew's my new boss.
He no longer thinks I'm off-limits...
And I no longer care that he's my dad's best friend.*

**But, will I regret letting my inhibitions get the best of me...
When I discover I'll become the mother of his baby?...
And when danger comes knocking...
Can my baby's father save us when we need him most?**

CHAPTER 1

BECCA

"Janey? Janey? Can you hear me?"

"Yeah, I can hear ya," her crackling voice called through the car's speakers. "Where are you?"

"I'm driving home. Be back in Boston in about half an hour."

"Hurry up! It's been forever since I've seen you."

"I know. I've missed you, bitch."

"Bitch, I missed you too!"

Up ahead, the traffic was gridlocked, and I braked to a halt watching the red lights of the cars in front glow through the rain. It was nearly Thanksgiving and the northeastern weather was dreary. Soon the snow would be falling, and Christmas lights would be going up.

"I can't believe you're moving back," Janey said.

I could hear her chewing and the sound was bugging me, but she was always nibbling on something. "Me neither, but I really think it's for the best, you know."

"Are you sure? I thought you had all those fancy plans of making it big as a personal trainer and building your own gym in New York."

"Yeah, well, that's not exactly a reality now, is it? I mean how am I supposed to do that? I just graduated from college and have no proper real-world experience. The gym will come. It's just not the right time."

"You think you'll get a personal trainer job when you're back in Boston?"

"That's the plan."

"You'll get one no problem. "

"God I hope so."

"Where do you reckon you'll go?" she asked with a crunch.

"I'm not really sure."

There were plenty of gyms near where I grew up that would be happy to hire someone as ambitious and hard working as me, but there was only one place I *wanted* to be.

"I wanna work for Matthew," I announced.

"Matthew? As in your dad's best friend?"

"Obviously. How many Matthews do I know that own a chain of nationwide gyms?"

We both giggled and I knew we were both thinking the same thing; working for Matthew was every girl's fantasy.

"Oh, my God, Becca, he's soooo hot," Janey cooed. At last, she'd stopped eating. "I saw his latest commercial on TV last night and... Jesus Christ, he's got buns that could crack walnuts. Don't let Harry know I said that, though."

Harry was her boyfriend, the love of her life, her knight in shining armor. They'd been together since they were seventeen and were still hopelessly in love. It made me want to puke seeing the two of them whisper sweet nothings into each other's ears and kiss like they'd just met. They were so sweet and sickly, just watching them put me at risk of getting diabetes.

In all the years she'd been with him, she'd never so much as looked at another guy, let alone commented on how hot they were. But that was the power Matthew had over women. He could make anyone fall for him.

Built like a Greek god with piercing blue eyes and bronzed skin, he towered over most people at six foot six and made any female he met melt. I'd had my eyes on him since I was a little girl, and my innocent admiration had turned into something more passionate, more forbidden, as I grew older.

Matthew was off limits to me for many reasons, and it wasn't just because he was my dad's best friend. He was also twenty years older than me and married. Until recently.

Six months ago he'd suffered through a very messy, very public divorce from his bitch of an ex-wife, Olivia, who was stupid enough to have an affair. It defied belief. How could anyone cheat on Matthew Banks, the hottest man alive?

From the tidbits of gossip I got from my dad, the affair had been going on for years, and of all the people she had to blow her marriage vows on, it had to be her accountant, Simon Grenville, a sniveling dweeb about a quarter of Matthew's size.

Olivia was a cold woman, and no one believed she was in love with the guy. She had to want something from him. Something that was worth losing Matthew for. It was soon revealed Simon came from a long line of Grenvilles who oozed old money charm and had fingers in every political pie in the country and access to all the finery and elegance Olivia desired: memberships at prestigious country clubs and vast estates of ancient properties that sprawled the Massachusetts landscapes, to name a couple.

Simon had relatives that reached the higher echelons of the political stratosphere. Soon it became evident that with Matthew, Olivia could be rich and glamorous, but with Simon, she was one step closer to being First Lady.

Still, I couldn't understand how she could have ruined

what she had with Matthew. It just didn't compute in my head that she had been lucky enough to marry him and choose someone else instead.

She's insane, I decided. *There can be no other reason.*

"You're right," I said to Jane. "He makes Brad Pitt look like a homeless bum."

"Brad Pitt?" she laughed. "What is it with you talking about old dudes?""

"What can I say? I appreciate a mature gentleman."

Up ahead, the traffic finally began to move. Stepping on the accelerator, I willed the journey to end as soon as possible. It had been an arduous day, starting off at six am to pack the last of my belongings before saying goodbye to New York, the city that had been my home for four years and the place I thought was my future.

But what did my future hold now? I had no idea. All I knew was that after all this time being independent, I was moving back in with my dad.

"So you wanna hang out tonight?" she asked.

"I dunno. I want to but I'm exhausted."

"No worries, we can get together tomorrow. We need to catch up, have some proper girly time together."

"Definitely."

"I can't wait! It's been so long since we've lived in the same town. It'll be just like back in the good old days. Just you and me, thick as thieves."

"And Harry," I trilled. It came out sounding more sarcastic than I meant and I worked to soften my tone. "I mean, I love Harry," I continued. "Couldn't imagine you without him."

"Me either," Jane swooned. "I feel so blessed having him. Like we were just meant to be together, like fate or some shit. We're actual soul mates."

Here we go again with the schmaltz.

"Yeah, you're a lucky girl," I said, changing lanes as I

moved into the fast-flowing traffic of the highway. "So when do you think he'll propose?"

"Who knows. I've been dropping hints for months! Sometimes I don't think we'll ever get married."

"Don't stress about it. It's just a piece of paper."

"Just a piece of paper! Wow, you're such a romantic."

I laughed and accelerated along the outside lane, eager to reach home as quickly as possible. All I wanted was to crash on the couch with Dad. Job applications and unpacking could be worried about in the morning.

"Anyway," she said, chewing again. "I gotta go. Harry will be home soon and I gotta put dinner on."

"You're such a dutiful little wifey," I laughed. "He better appreciate all you do for him."

"Oh, he knows how to say thank you once dessert's been served and..."

"Alright, spare the details. I'll call you in the morning."

"You better. Love ya!"

"Love ya, too."

I reached over to switch off the hands free. The car was plunged into silence with only the sound of the wet asphalt beneath us as the tires drove through the rain.

Just ten more minutes and I'll be home, I thought to myself as I yawned.

As I drove, I thought of Matthew again. What were the chances of getting to work for him? Minimal probably, but I could always dream. And I'd always dreamed about him. He was my first crush, the first guy I'd ever met who gave me that creamy tingling sensation between my legs.

I'd never forget the time in high school when our basketball coach broke his leg a month before the championship. Suddenly we went from being a team with a chance of winning it big time to being a team that would have to forfeit everything. Without a coach, we were nothing.

But Matthew decided to step in. He knew all about the practices my dad used to drive me to and how hard I'd worked. So when it looked as though our team wouldn't be able to compete, he decided the only way to save the day was to step in and coach us himself.

We'd all been standing outside the girls' locker room commiserating on the fate of the team when he appeared at the end of the hall with the assistant coach we loved but who didn't really know anything about basketball. Carrying a sack of basketballs, Matthew arrived like a guardian angel in tight fitting shorts and a tank top that showed off his bulging muscles.

For a second, all the girls just stared, shocked into silence, then one by one they began to blush and giggle. But I'd kept my cool and just nodded to him, trying to look as nonchalant as possible even though my insides were melting.

"Sup?" I'd said as he approached me. "So my old man told you about the team."

"He told me everything. Thought I'd get you to the championship myself."

All the girls on the team were staring at me with their eyes like saucers. I knew what they were all thinking. *How the hell does she know him?* I pretended it was no big deal.

He fit into the slot of coach easily, and for the first time in the team's history, every single player turned up to every single practice session, and they were even early. In fact, practice began earlier and earlier every day as people practically sprinted from their last class to get to Matthew's sessions.

And something else unusual started to happen. The girls' moms started to tag along just to watch. They'd stand up on the bleachers pretending they were there to support their little girls. But we all knew they just wanted to see Matthew running around getting all sweaty. And who could blame them?

On the day of the championship game, the place was packed. You would have thought LeBron James himself was playing. But as I dribbled down the court, I became aware that no one was watching me because all eyes were on Matthew.

We'd sailed through the final and become state champions. After bringing us to victory, Matthew left his post as substitute and a few months later, our old coach, who had the charm, looks, and personality of a potato in comparison, returned. Half the girls quit the team, and the school hadn't won the state championship again.

But for me, the real joy didn't come from winning, although I had loved seeing my hard work pay off. It had come from going home and dreaming of him, of thinking of all the multiple ways we could become even closer. I used to make excuses to not shower at school so I could go home and run the hottest bath to have even hotter dreams. As the steam rose in the room, I'd sink my fingers between my legs and imagine Matthew's strong body.

He'd built his wealth on being able to sculpt people's bodies into perfection, but his was the most perfect of all. There wasn't an inch of fat anywhere on him, and his skin was the color of caramel. Then there was his face. Square-jawed and blue eyed with cheekbones that could cut glass. He could make a gal flood her panties with just a look. Not that he ever looked at me as anything more than the daughter of his best friend. No matter how much I stared at him and willed him to notice me, he didn't so much as glance in my direction unless it was to give me advice on my dribbling.

But he didn't look at any of the girls or their mothers. He was a one-woman guy, and although people gossiped and imagined what a little extra coaching from him would be like, he couldn't have been more respectful to any of us. Despite being surrounded by a team of girls, he behaved like a saint.

But I didn't want a saint. I wanted him to be bad, and I couldn't stop the rampant fantasies about him in my mind. As I lay in the bath, I'd fantasize about him taking me to the side during practice with one of his strong hands gripping my wrist.

"You need some extra practice," he'd tell me in his gruff, low voice. "It looks like I'll have to give you some one-on-one drills after the rest of the team leaves."

The thought sent me reeling as I imagined the court emptying, leaving just the two of us. But soon, thoughts of basketball would disappear, and he'd be sliding his hands down my sides and pulling me toward him.

"I can teach you things," he'd murmur before pushing his lips against mine.

The fantasy always ended the same way, with him taking my hand and leading me into the empty locker room where he'd lift me in his strong arms and press me up against the wall. With my legs around his waist, he'd fuck me slowly and lovingly, but firmly. He would take control and dominate me, but his eyes would always be fixed on mine.

I'd had my first orgasm to this, then my second and third and hundredth.

Even when I grew older and moved away to college, where I met boys my own age and started to date, my mind always drifted back to him. Nobody ever came close to him, and as short-lived relationships blossomed and dwindled, one after the other, I came to the realization that subconsciously, I was holding out for him. Always hoping that somehow, at some point, he would be the one I ended up with.

But I knew how ridiculous that was. He would never be

interested in someone like me. He probably still remembered me as the snotty nosed tomboy who used to run around the yard playing ball with all the neighborhood kids.

Back then, I was indistinguishable from most of the boys on the block. I loved sports, never wore pretty dresses or makeup and my idea of a good weekend was getting muddy and running around with the dogs. I was nothing compared to Olivia. But then again, I wouldn't want to be.

At last, just as my eyelids grew heavy, I could see the roof of my dad's house as I turned into the street.

"Jesus..."

The place looked scruffy as hell and the leaves had clearly not been raked in weeks. Meanwhile, the garage had spilled its guts and there were bits of cars and gym equipment littering the drive. As I climbed out of the car and stretched my legs, I sighed heavily.

"Don't look so happy to be here," Dad's sarcastic voice called from the porch. He was standing in the doorway with a beer in his hand and his gym clothes still on.

"Dad " I ran up the steps and threw my arms around him. "Aw, it's good to be back."

"You're looking great, kiddo," he said, kissing my cheek.

"Yeah, well, I can't say the same for this place. Looks like a bomb went off."

"Yeah, I keep meaning to tidy up but..." He took a sip of his drink and motioned for me to enter the hall. "Since when do you care about cleaning up?"

"And since when did you start drinking beer? I thought you only liked a single malt on special occasions."

"Yeah well, since Matthew's been free and single, he's kinda been gettin' your old man back out in the bars again. Think I'm getting a taste for this Budweiser shit."

"Well, don't get too much of a taste for it. Mom hated Budweiser. She said it tasted like pee."

He laughed and wrapped his arm around me. "God you sound just like her," he announced. "And you look more and more like her each time I see you too."

We walked into the lounge and fell silent. Her picture was framed on the fireplace, looking at us. For a second, I imagined she was in the kitchen cooking dinner. When I was younger, I used to stand in front of that photo and talk to it as though she was there. But she wasn't. She hadn't been since I was seven, when she had succumbed to the breast cancer that had ravaged her body.

I took a seat on the armchair by the window and looked up at her photo. *Oh, Mom, if you could see the state of this place.*

Just like my dad, she had been a fitness fanatic and had meticulously high standards in everything she did, from working out to cleaning the house to cooking a dynamite dinner.

She would not have been impressed with the house and what Dad had let it become in her absence. I reached over to the coffee table and ran my fingers through the thick layer of dust.

"First thing tomorrow, we're cleaning the shit outta this place," I said to myself, but Dad heard me from the doorway.

He had set down his beer and replaced it with a coffee for him and a hot chocolate for me.

"Wow, that was quick," I smiled, taking the cup gratefully from his hand. "You must have had it waiting for me."

"Hey, I remember how my little girl likes her hot chocolate. Especially after a long journey."

He sat on the couch across the table from me. Beside him, the television screen flickered on his face. There was an old ball game playing, a re-run from the nineties and I paid it little attention. I was too busy looking at the electric light shine across his face and how old he seemed to me.

He had always been one of the cool, young dads, the kind

that let you stay up late and eat all the candy at Halloween. And he was always the first guy to help out with school activities. But now, he looked exhausted, just a shadow of what I remembered.

"Dad, are you okay? You look tired."

"Been putting in extra hours down at the gym."

Just like Matthew, he had also become a personal trainer, but instead of being the multi-millionaire fitness and nutrition tycoon Matthew had become, he'd opted for a humbler career path. After my mom passed, he took on a small, run-down boxing gym and took just about every position in the place from janitor to boxing coach to tax man.

At first, keeping busy had benefited him. It gave him something to focus on and distracted him from the grief, but now I was starting to wonder if he should take some time out and relax.

"Anyway," he said, sipping his milky coffee. "I don't wanna talk about me. I wanna hear about you! I can't believe you're back, Becca."

"Neither can I," I replied with a roll of the eyes.

"Don't be like that. It'll be great for you here. Boston's where your roots are. It's where you belong."

"I know. I know. I really love the place. Really think I can make a go of it," I said, smiling slowly. "As long as I can get a job."

There was a weird glint in his eyes as if he was holding back a secret. "And where are you thinking of working?"

"A gym, obviously. I'd love to work my way up from personal trainer to business owner, just like you, Dad."

He smiled and his cheeks flushed with warmth. "Any gym in mind?" I shrugged. "What about that one gym you always talked about when you were younger?" There was that mischievous look in his eyes again.

"What? Matthew's gym?" I asked.

He nodded. "Remember what your dream used to be?"

I looked into my chocolate and thought of Matthew. *Would I see him again now that I was back?* I was bound to at some point.

Was he still as hot as I thought he was?
Was he still as cheeky and fun to be around?
Or had he aged badly like my tired dad?

"My dream..." I mused.

"You used to say you'd love to make it into corporate at Matthew's company so you could be in charge of making all the big decisions. You used to say you'd like him to expand away from all his celebrity clients and target everyday people. Do you remember that?"

"Sure, I remember. But that was just some silly dream I had," I said, trying to play it down. "It's not like it's going to actually happen."

The look on his face intensified until it looked as though he was ready to burst.

"Why are you looking at me like that?" I asked.

"Like what?"

"Like you're going to explode."

He stood up and walked over to me, the light from the television flickering on the newly formed gray hairs on his head.

"Becca," he said, sitting on the arm of the chair beside me. "I was talking to Matthew last night. He knows you're coming back and that you need a job, so..."

"So?" My heartbeat began to quicken.

"So, I asked if he could help you out. Lord knows I've helped him out over the years."

"And what did he say?" I asked with a touch too much enthusiasm.

"He said the least he could do for me was give my little girl a job interview. "

At first, I thought he had to be joking. Could I really be so lucky to land an interview for a position in Matthew's office?

"Anyway," Dad said, slapping his hand onto my shoulder. "He's known you your whole life and he knows how smart you are."

I sat dazed for a second. I'd had interviews in the past for temp jobs while I was at college, and they always made me anxious. But an interview with Matthew? That was something else entirely! It was both nerve wracking and exciting. I'd get to see his office, and I'd get to be face to face with him for the first time in years.

Immediately my mind fell into the gutter. I imagined walking into his office only for him to ask me a series of naughty interview questions.

"Honey?" Dad interrupted my thoughts. "Are you okay?"

I realized I'd been staring at the TV with my mouth dropped open like a fish. "Yeah," I replied. "I'm just a little nervous."

CHAPTER 2

MATTHEW

"Oof," grunted my assistant, Sandra, as she staggered into my office.

She was getting bigger by the day and waddled to my desk with her iPad in her hands. Her previously pale, thin face was now full and rosy, and her hair, which used to be tied up in a tight bun most of the time, hung loose around her shoulders.

"Sandra, I told you to take time off," I said to her as she perched on the edge of my sleek, black glass desk. "It's ridiculous, you coming into work every day when you're seven months pregnant."

"What am I supposed to do? Go home and put my feet up?"

"Yes, that's literally exactly what you're supposed to do."

She waved her hand dismissively at me and flicked through files on her iPad. "That sounds like hell," she said. "I hate being stuck at home. It's too boring. I'd rather be here getting on with things."

"You'll have to take time off eventually."

"Yeah, when the baby drops."

"Well, I hope you don't drop it on this carpet. Just had it steam cleaned." She gave me a look, one eyebrow arched as I chuckled. "Look," I said, leaning toward her. "You've been with me since the start. You're not just my assistant, you're..."

"Like a sister?"

"I was going to say friend, but sure. You're like my little sister, I suppose. I don't want you working too much when you should be thinking of the baby. Please, promise me after this week you'll take some time off."

She looked back down at the screen and said, "I'll think about it. Besides, the holidays are coming up. I'll get a short break then."

I nodded, knowing full well that she'd spend the holidays cooking like she always did.

"Anyway," she said, clearly ending the conversation. "You've got a busy day ahead of you. Wanna hear the schedule?"

"Shoot."

"Okay, so your first meeting of the day is with Gigi Deloma at nine thirty."

I looked up at the clock and saw it was twenty past already

"But she's always late," Sandra added.

"True."

"After that, you've got a meeting with Eddie Goldwyn."

"Goldwyn? Already? I wasn't supposed to meet him until Friday."

"He called first thing this morning. Pretty much forced me to slot him in today."

"Shit!"

That didn't sound good. It had been two months since I put forward the plan to buy the Goldwyn chain of gyms. As far as I was concerned, we had a few minor things to smooth out before the big day on Friday when we finally shook hands on the deal. But he was here today? Something about that felt all wrong.

I knew Goldwyn. Not only was he my idol growing up, but he was my closest business competitor. I had studied him closely and knew that he didn't make decisions lightly or rush a meeting. Whatever he was here to talk about had to be important.

"Who's after him?" I asked Sandra.

"You're interviewing for the position of operations consultant with a woman named Becca Canmore?"

Becca, I thought. She had been such a sweet kid, and it had been years since I'd seen her. The last time had been when she was packing her things to move away to college. I could barely believe she was that age already, but time flew like a motherfucker.

When I'd seen her dad, Bob, last night, he'd said she was back in town and borderline desperate to get a job in fitness. He mentioned she had some big ideas to share with me and that he thought she would be a great employee.

On the spur of the moment, I'd told him to bring her along to an interview. I wasn't sure if I could hire her, but an interview wouldn't hurt. Bob had been my best buddy for over two decades, and I'd watched Becca grow up from being the apple of her dad's eye to a basketball champion and now a college graduate.

The least I could do was give Becca a chance and interview her. She might even be a good fit at the company. Not to mention if Bob hadn't helped me through my finals in college, I wouldn't even have the career I had now.

From outside in the waiting room where Sandra's desk sat, a buzzer sounded.

"That'll be Gigi," she said, sliding off my desk with a groan.

"I doubt it. She's never on time for anything. Pretty sure she was late to her own birth."

"She'd be early for you," Sandra laughed as she pressed the button for the door. "She can't take her eyes off you. I reckon she's got you in mind as her next ex-husband."

"Don't say that. I couldn't find anything less appealing than lying next to her plastic ass every night."

"Ouch!"

It sounded harsh but I meant it. She was the fakest woman I'd ever met; more silicone than human. The majority of men found her attractive, and why wouldn't they? She was a celebrity pop star, the hottest thing since Britney Spears. But for some reason, she was as sexually appealing to me as a wet fish and had a worse personality.

"That's her coming in just now," Sandra told me.

I rose from my seat, ready to welcome her. She sauntered in with her entourage in tow: two bodyguards, a life coach who followed her everywhere to help her manage her anxiety, and her manager, a squat man named Bertie in a white suit.

Gigi herself stood just under five foot five even in her high heels and was clad head to toe in fur. Even her boots were made from what I recognized from Olivia's wardrobe as rabbit.

"Matthew dahling!" she cooed and gave me an air kiss.

I reached out to shake her hand, and she slipped her icy fingers between mine.

"What's the need for formality?" she asked, sliding off her sunglasses to reveal her pale blue eyes lined with thick makeup. I couldn't help but notice on either side of her nose were two small bruises from where she'd recently had fillers.

"I'm so excited to be here," she trilled, taking a seat while her entourage gathered behind her. My office was by no means small, but with everyone packed around my desk, it felt cramped.

"Sandra, some drinks in here, please?"

She nodded and departed, returning a few moments later with a tray of sparkling water.

"So," Gigi said, picking at her long fingernails. "How's the campaign going?"

It was a simple question, but I didn't have a simple answer. Six months ago, all the big boys in corporate decided that a great way to boost publicity would be to place some of our celebrity clients in the commercials with before and after shots of their bodies.

"People will go nuts for it!" one of my consultants, Alan, had told me. "It'll pull in the big bucks, I swear!"

It had sounded like a solid plan, except the results hadn't been what we'd expected. We got all the biggest names we could muster from our client books, actors, singers, models, and sports stars, and plastered their images beside our name. But for some reason, the public wasn't biting. If anything, it looked as though they were put off by our new advertising strategy. And from the feedback we'd collected from the public, it looked as though Gigi's commercial was the least popular of all.

"She's so annoying!" one viewer commented.

"She looks so fake!"

"We know her body wasn't built in the gym. It was created on the operating table."

And so it went on.

People might love watching Gigi up on stage, but they hated her in our gym. But how was I supposed to tell her that?

"I'm afraid," I began, choosing my words carefully, "that it wouldn't be the most efficient strategy to see the campaign into the next phase of proceedings."

"What does that mean?" she asked, whipping her neck and pointing her nails at me.

"It means he's dropping you from the campaign," Bertie announced harshly. "An unwise decision, if you ask me."

"Not unwise," I replied. "Just sensible regarding our market feedback."

"I hate all you business boys and your jargon," Bertie spat. "Come on, Gigi. We've well and truly wasted our time here."

He stood up to leave, gesturing for the rest of the group to follow him out. Everyone trotted out after him except for Gigi. She hung back until it was just the two of us in the room and sauntered over, swaying her hips.

"You can't really be dropping me from the campaign," she purred, sitting on the edge of my desk and leaning over to push her cleavage in my face. Her platinum blonde hair extensions fell across my face, and I swiped them out the way.

"I'm sorry our working relationship couldn't have ended under more agreeable circumstances."

"I love it when you say big words," she said, licking her glossy lips. "Say something else."

I just stared at her.

"Look," she said. "I get it. You don't really wanna drop me, but the big guys in suits are pressuring you to do what they tell you. I get that all the time. If it ain't Bertie telling me what to wear for the fans, then the producers are telling me to do this and that and sometimes I end up making decisions that don't feel like they're my decision at all. You get me?"

"Yes," I said, watching her lean even closer to me.

"Anyway," she continued. "Just because our little campaign together has ended doesn't mean that you and me can't..."

I lifted an eyebrow rather than acknowledge her obvious hint.

"You know, still hang out. Have some fun. The Emmys are this weekend. Would you like to be my plus one?"

"Thanks, but no. I have plans."

"What could be more important than going to the Emmys with me?" she asked, offended.

"I've got a night out planned with my best pal," I told her.

"Pffft. Come with me instead."

"I appreciate the offer, but no."

Standing up, I walked over to the door and held it for her, willing her to leave. When she continued to sprawl herself out across my desk, I yelled to Sandra.

"Sandra, see Gigi out, will you?"

She appeared in the doorway immediately, ready to escort the pop star out of my office.

"You're missing out," Gigi said as she strutted past, hitting me with her handbag as she left. "Just to let you know, Gigi doesn't give second chances. "

I burst out laughing, a response she wasn't expecting. "Okay, bye now. Have a nice day."

She walked away, seething.

"So, that went well," Sandra laughed. "I told you she was into you. Although it sounds as though you're not getting another chance."

"I don't want it," I chuckled. "I'm pretty sure I just dodged a bullet."

"Eddie! Good to see you!" As I walked into the board room, I saw the sentiment wasn't shared. His face was as warm as granite, his eyes dark and unwelcoming.

"Hello," he said, rising to shake my hand.

"Thank you for coming earlier than expected. Can I get you anything?"

"No, your lovely assistant took care of me. Now, shall we sit down and discuss business?"

Wow, that was abrupt. What's he in a hurry about?

I sat across from him, the two of us alone in the vast space of the room that normally housed a dozen of the top members of the corporate sector. They had wanted to be there, of course, but I found their presence irritating. I liked to talk business face to face like a man and not hide behind a team of suits.

"Yes, let's discuss the matter at hand," I said, leaning back in my seat to feign a relaxed demeanor.

Usually nothing ruffled my feathers, but I had to admit as I sat in front of Eddie Goldwyn, a man I had admired since childhood, I felt my palms begin to sweat. It was he who had been the inspiration behind my career in the first place, the guy I had modeled myself after.

But he wasn't the spritely athlete I had adored decades ago. Now he was older and spent more time in the office than he did in the gym. Yet he still held a youthful, fiery appearance with his red hair coiffed to perfection and his posture strong and commanding.

"I'll be honest," I told him. "I wasn't expecting to see you so soon. I'd assumed that perhaps you'd have some more thinking to do on certain matters and—"

He raised a hand to silence me. "I'm sorry, but I'm going to just come out and say it."

Annoyed at him for interrupting me, I crossed my arms over my chest and frowned. "Say what?"

He ran a hand through his greased back hair, sighed, and said, "The board voted against the sale. They simply don't want it."

"But the decision is entirely up to you," I reminded him.

"As far as I remember, you own Goldwyn gyms, not the board."

He shook his head again and looked me up and down as though I was just some stupid kid with a head full of pipe dreams. "You and I both know that's not how business works. If the board says no, then the answer is no."

"Bullshit," I stated. "This sale was already set in motion. I had your word, Eddie."

"My word," he laughed and gave me a pitiful look.

I was sick of the way he talked to me, like I was nothing but an upstart compared to him, an old sage who had been in the business a lifetime. Never in my life had I felt the urge to hit an old man, but I felt as though I could have made an exception.

Eager to burn off the anger, I rose quickly and walked over to the window so I didn't have to look at his smug face.

"You really let me down," I told him, forcing my voice to remain calm. "This could have benefited both of us tremendously. Your board has made an enormous mistake."

He said nothing, but I could hear him slurping his tea.

At the window, I looked out across the Boston skyline. I could see a few of my gyms dotting the cityscape, their blue and green lights glittering among all the brown brick. But there should have been more of them where Eddie's gyms now stood.

I tried to fathom why he was being such a difficult old bastard. Didn't he want me to buy him out? Didn't he want to be rich? Surely, he couldn't go on working as he did, not at his age.

Then I thought of the board he spoke of. The faceless suits that made all the decisions for him.

Assholes, I thought. *What the fuck do they know?*

Then it dawned on me.

They may not know shit about running gyms, but they knew the language of money.

"It's the shares, isn't it?" I wondered aloud, still looking out the window. "They're still shareholders, so if I buy you out, they won't be able to cash in on the price hike after the acquisition."

Behind me, Eddie spun around in his seat, still sipping on his tea. "You're too smart for your own good," he said, setting the dainty cup down on the saucer with a clink. "I'm sorry things couldn't have worked out between us."

"I'm sorry, too, for wasting my time on you."

He set the cup and saucer on the table, unfazed by my insult, and said, "Have a good day, Mr. Banks. I trust I'll be seeing more of your commercials on the television."

And just like that, he walked away, closing the door with a click as he departed.

"Bastard!" I raged now that I was alone. The buyout should have gone smoothly. His gyms would be mine and Banks Fitness would be double the size it was now. But how could my dream turn to shit so quickly?

I wanted to punch a wall, but instead, I smoothed my suit, took a deep breath, and pressed the button for Sandra's desk.

"The meeting with Eddie is over," I said. "Bring a scotch on ice over to my office, will you?"

"Certainly."

As I walked to my office, she was already setting it down on my desk. When she saw my face, her eyes crinkled with concern.

"Not good news, I take it."

"No," I said, taking a sip of scotch and grimacing at its strength. "But fuck it. There'll be more opportunities to grow. This is nothing but a blip on the horizon. Won't be long until Eddie realizes what a mistake he made. "

Lunchtime came and went, and I was still reeling from the bombshell Eddie had dropped. I didn't want to be angry, but I couldn't help it. I'd been eyeing his gyms for months now, and never for a second did I think I wouldn't get them. But bureaucracy, as usual, got in the way?

I sat at my desk, sipping an espresso, trying to calm my anger.

I'd worked so fucking hard to get to where I was, and I was so close to getting to where I needed to be. But then Eddie had to throw a wrench in the works and hold me back. I shouldn't have taken it so badly. Business was a fickle mistress and temperamental at the best of times. I had to admit that I couldn't always get everything to go my way, but I couldn't help but feel a swell of rage. I may have been a hard worker, but since the divorce, I'd thrown myself into overdrive trying to make the company grow to newer heights. Yet it wasn't growing at all. If anything, things were moving backward.

I didn't get it. I'd built this place from the ground up using nothing but tried and tested traditional business strategies that always worked. So why weren't they working now? Why was our latest advertising campaign failing? Why couldn't we take over Goldwyn's, for Christ's sake! It should have been a done and dusted deal!

My head was spinning when I heard a knock on the door. "Yes?"

"It's your interview candidate," Sandra's voice announced as she opened the door. "Becca Canmore."

Conducting an interview was the last thing I wanted to do, and if it was anyone but Becca, I might have considered canceling. But now that she was there, there was no harm in seeing her.

"Sure, let her in," I said, sighing.

From the foyer, I heard the click of heels on the marble floor, and a second later a figure appeared in the doorway. At first, I wondered who the hell the model was who had stumbled into my office. Then I realized she was no model.

"Becca! Wow, I almost didn't recognize you."

The last time I'd seen her she was in jeans and a hoodie, carrying boxes to her car. But here she was in a tight pencil skirt that hugged her curvy hips, a tight-fitting blouse that accentuated her large, round breasts, and black stilettos. Her face, though free from makeup, was glowing and her skin was radiant. And her previously short hair was now long and flowing down her back.

"You look great!" I blurted out before I could stop myself. "I mean, you look so grown up now. Please, take a seat."

Fuck, she's gorgeous, I thought. *This is not what I expected.*

Appearing confident, she sat down elegantly in front of my desk and crossed her legs. "Thank you for seeing me," she said, her voice no longer babyish but mature, almost husky.

"You're very welcome."

Sitting back down at my desk, I noticed her legs were pointing in my direction, her skirt riding up her thigh to reveal the shapely form of her muscles.

Take your eyes off her! She's your best friend's daughter!

But I couldn't stop myself. It was like I was being faced with a stranger, As though the Becca I used to know was long gone and replaced with this absolute goddess.

"Okay, so your dad told me you have some ideas," I began. "He said you don't want to waste your time in the gym with all the other trainers. That you want to make it up to corporate."

"That makes me sound like an arrogant brat," she laughed, her voice filling the room. "What I actually meant was that I'd eventually like to progress up through the company, not just spend every day sweating it out with the clients."

"So you'd like to be here for the long haul?"

"Absolutely," she replied positively with a nod of her head. "I don't flake out."

I could see that. She may have been dressed femininely, but there was no denying the strength of her body, a body that had been crafted through hours in the gym and sheer sweat and determination.

She could be the face of the company, I thought to myself. *She'd sell a million more memberships than that nightmare Gigi.*

"So tell me some of your ideas," I encouraged. "Your dad told me you've got plenty."

A slight look of nervousness flashed across her face, then it vanished as she began to talk. "Okay, so I've been studying your company for a while now."

"You have?"

"Yes. At college we had to do a module on sports business management, and I chose Banks Fitness as my case study for my assignment."

"Wow. Impressive."

"Your company really stands out because you focus on a high-class clientele from a celebrity background. You're luxury all the way. Your prices are high, your clients are the biggest and baddest, and your gyms are synonymous with the celebrity lifestyle that everyone craves. But I think you're missing something."

"What's that?" I asked, leaning forward eagerly.

She was on the ball, the words tumbling out her mouth as though she'd rehearsed them a thousand times. She looked as though she gave pitches like this every day of her life.

"You're missing out on folk like me, on the wannabees, the students, the millennials who want a million-dollar body on a Dollar Tree budget."

I sat back in my seat and let her words sink in.

"I know what you're thinking," she said. "That I'm nuts. That the whole point of your business is that it's high end and luxurious. That you don't want to stoop to a lower demographic. But tell me this, how many celebrities are there?"

I shrugged.

"Thousands, right?" she said. "But do you know who there are more of? People who *want* to be celebrities. For every Gigi, there's a thousand girls on Instagram wanting to be just like her. And that means getting access to all the things she has. The clothes, the makeup, the body..."

"The gym membership..."

Shit. She's really onto something.

"I mean, think about it. Remember when Maseratis were only for millionaires, but now you can lease them monthly. Every damned neighborhood has some guy whizzing about the streets in one of those things. It didn't hurt them to target the little man, did it?"

She uncrossed her legs and leaned forward, her hands moving animatedly as she spoke.

"I know you're thinking I'm just some jumped up college kid with her head in the clouds. And you'd have every right. But I really think I can show you an angle you're missing. A way to reach a new demographic that's uncharted territory for you."

For a second I was stunned. In all my years in the industry, I'd never interviewed someone with so much confidence and belief in themselves. I was impressed by her, that was for sure. And not just with the way she spoke but in the way she carried herself and the effortless grace and glamour that oozed out of her.

What struck me the most was that she probably didn't even care that she wasn't wearing makeup or that her hair wasn't styled in the latest fashion. It was as though she didn't even know how good she looked. All she wanted was to talk business, and, my God, there was nothing sexier than a woman with her business hat on.

But at the same time, I had to think rationally. I couldn't just give her a job because she had the gift of gab, and I definitely couldn't give her a job because she was hot as hell. Then there was the matter of her being Bob's little girl. I never was one to indulge in nepotism and had always believed people had to earn their place in a company. So did Becca deserve a place at Banks Fitness? I was in two minds.

"I appreciate you coming in today," I told her. "You definitely have a lot of strong ideas. I'll be in touch as soon as I make a decision."

Looking disappointed, she narrowed her eyes and said, "Oh."

The slump of her shoulders as she stood showed she felt rejected. She knew what *I'll be in touch* meant. But the look in her eyes said *fuck you. I don't need your job anyway*. And I didn't doubt that if I didn't give her a position, someone else would in a heartbeat.

"Well, thank you for your time," she said, shaking my hand.

I couldn't help but notice she wasn't wearing the long, acrylic talons so many women like Olivia and Gigi wore, but had opted for clipped, unpolished nails. They were no-nonsense hands. Hands that lifted weights and worked hard. But despite the lack of girly finishings, her skin was silky soft and warm to the touch. And I found myself holding onto her hand for a moment longer than necessary.

"Goodbye, Matthew," she said. She held my gaze for a second, smiled, then left. I watched her walk away with her head held high, her shoulders back, and her gait smooth and balanced.

"Wow," Sandra said as she watched Becca disappear into the elevator. "That girl makes Gigi look like an old fishwife."

"Doesn't she just?" I said, still feeling the silken touch of her hand in mine. "She'd make a Victoria's Secret model look average."

CHAPTER 3

BECCA

"Sup bitch!"
"How did the interview go?"
"Ugh."
"That good, eh?"
"It was a freakin' disaster."
"Tell me everything."

I was lying in bed staring at the ceiling. The room had remained untouched since I moved away to college. My cheesy boy band posters were still on the walls. At one end of the room were my sports trophies from school, piled high in a pyramid so they took up an entire wall to themselves. On the other end were all my sketchbooks and diaries, meticulously filed away in chronological order. Nobody had really seen any of them, not even Dad. Only Janey had seen some of my drawings and poetry I'd created in the privacy of my own room when I couldn't sleep.

Everything I penned was about my mom, and I saw my art journals and diaries as a way to communicate with her, saying all the things I couldn't. The juxtaposition of the diaries on one end of the room and the trophies on the other was a stark contrast that portrayed the binary opposites of my personality. Competitive, sporty, and practical at one of the spectrum and soft, creative, and sensitive at the other. Between the two sat my bed where I lay now, commiserating as I stared into Justin Timberlake's eyes.

"I fucked up," I told Janey. "I was so nervous that I tried to pretend I was all confident and ended up coming across as a total douche."

"Shut up. I bet you didn't."

"No, I really did. I basically went in, sat down, and told him how I could make his company better. I mean seriously! Could I be any more embarrassing?"

"But that's what you wanted to do, wasn't it? Tell him all about your ideas for the company, right?"

"Yeah, but not like that."

"So what did he say?"

"That he'd *be in touch*."

"That's it?"

"That's it," I said. "He'd be in touch. That basically means no, right?" I asked.

Janey was ominously silent. "Not exactly," she eventually said.

"Give me a break. That's exactly what it means. If he wanted to give me a job, he would have been like 'awesome, you start tomorrow'. But no. He couldn't have shown me the door quick enough."

"You're probably looking too much into it," Janey said. "I bet it went fine. You're worrying about nothing." She scoffed. "You're always like this. If you don't get things perfect the first time you start freaking out."

"That's true. But I just can't shake the feeling I messed up."

"So what? Everyone messes up from time to time."

"Not me."

That wasn't exactly true. No one was right all the time.

But generally, I threw myself headfirst into a task with as much energy as I could gather and gave it my all. Sometimes, my over enthusiasm would bite me on the ass, like the interview with Matthew. He probably thought I was a cocky bitch, strutting in there and telling him to change demographics and target new audiences.

"Okay, but enough about the interview," Janey said, interrupting my thoughts. "Is he as hot as you remembered?"

"Oh, my God, he's like ten times hotter! Seriously, the second I walked in there, my heart was beating like a hummingbird's. Age has treated him well," I told her, sighing longingly. "He's got to be one of those mythical people who look better the older they get. He even has these little gray hairs poking out the sides of his temples, and they are just frigging adorable."

"Oooh, like Richard Gere in *Pretty Woman?*"

"He's ten times hotter than Richard Gere."

But there was something else I'd noticed about his appearance. The last time I'd seen him, he was a bouncing ball of energy and ambition, and although at the interview he presented himself as his usual alpha self with an iron disposition, there was a hint of exhaustion behind his eyes. Like he was jaded by life. Like he needed to get the hell out the office and have some fun.

I could show him a good time, I thought. *He could do with a young thing like me to zap that tiredness right out of him. And I sure as shit wouldn't mess him around like that bitch Olivia did.*

"So when do you think you'll get your answer from him?" Janey asked.

"Who knows," I sighed. "It could be next week or next month. Either way, not knowing is driving me nuts."

"I reckon you should just forget all about it for a night."

"How the hell am I supposed to do that? I can't think about anything else."

"By coming out with me and Harry," she proposed. "Come on. We'll hit a few bars, head to the clubs, dance the night away."

"Hmmm...I dunno."

"Aw come on! You used to love going out dancing. Just you and me and the dance floor."

"Yeah, but it's not just you and me anymore, is it? Harry will be there."

"Do I detect a touch of bitterness in your voice?"

"Not at all. I'm just saying I'll be a total third wheel all night."

"Aw, don't be like that. Come out with us. It'll be fun and we can play matchmaker for you."

"No. You're always trying to hook me up with guys."

"I just want you to be happy!" Janey moaned. "I mean, what's wrong with you getting a boyfriend?"

"I have absolutely zero time for a boyfriend right now."

"You've been saying that for months!" she grumbled. "You need to learn to have a little fun. I'm not saying you have to get into some serious relationship. But what's wrong with just fooling around?"

Nothing, except fooling around wasn't my style.

In college I'd had a few boyfriends, if you could even call them that. We'd hang out, go on a few dates, and maybe share a few kisses, but that's as far as it went.

The truth was that I just hadn't met anyone I truly connected with, and as for all the passion and fire in my loins I was supposed to feel, no guy I'd met had caused any of that.

As far as Janey and all my other friends were concerned, I was a regular young woman with the normal needs and urges I was expected to have. What they didn't know was that even though I had just had my twenty-third birthday, and although I had grown accustomed to receiving my fair share of male attention, I was actually a virgin.

It wasn't something I sat down and made a decision about, and it definitely wasn't for religious or moral reasons. Put simply, I just hadn't met anyone who rang my bell the way Matthew always had. Maybe it was stupid to wait for someone who turned me on the way he did, but I'd done it anyway. I was worth that, wasn't I?

"Let's meet for lunch tomorrow," I said. "And you and Harry have a great time tonight."

"Sure I can't tempt you to come out?"

I was still staring at the ceiling but wasn't focused on a thing. In my mind I was thinking of Matthew and how good he looked in his suit. And how domineering and in control he appeared in his luxurious office.

"Not tonight," I replied.

"Booo. If you change your mind, text me."

"I will. Have a good night. Love ya."

I hung up and imagined Matthew's face above me, his solid, muscular body weighing me down. My hand made its way south, my fingers slipping beneath the waistband of my jeans. As I remembered all those fantasies I'd had as a teenager, all those times I'd lain exactly like this with my hand between my legs thinking of him. I thought I'd never find anyone as sexy as him.

CHAPTER 4

MATTHEW

I entered Bob's gym and was instantly hit by the masculine smell of old school gyms I hadn't caught a whiff of in years sweat, testosterone, gym mats, and dirty socks.

I prided myself on having the cleanest, most up to date establishments with free toiletries in the locker rooms and a team of cleaners that kept the place immaculate every day. Bob's gym, on the other hand, looked as though it hadn't seen even the sweep of a broom in years.

Walking into the main room, I noted the boxing ring sat in the center below a sky light. I watched as young boys sparred in each corner while in the center, a young fella no older than sixteen was attempting to knock seven shades of shit out of another kid who was built like a tank. The sound of gloves smacking skin and their grunts filled the room.

"Yo, Matthew!" Bob called from the doorway to his office. "How's it goin'?"

"Good, man. Good. Still up for a beer?"

"It'll be a quick one. Got a ton of shit to do around here."

Entering his office, I saw a boxy room filled to the brim with gym equipment, sweaty clothes, and empty tins of protein shake. Among the clutter lay his cheap plasterboard desk that was covered in piles of paper.

"Whoa," I mumbled.

It had only been a few months since the last time I'd been there, but the mess had grown exponentially. Pulling a banana peel off the seat, I tossed it in the trash and sat down. Bob landed heavily in his creaky office chair and turned to his computer. Like everything else, I had the best computers money could buy, but Bob? His old, grimy PC looked as though it might have been an original.

"Bob?"

"Uh uh..."

"What the fuck is that?"

"What, this?"

"No, that," I said, pointing to the sheet of plastic sticking out of the computer's tower.

"It's a floppy disk."

I paused for a second and let my brain process what he'd said. "I'm sorry, Bob. For a second there I was sure you just said the words floppy disk."

"That's exactly what I said. What's wrong with still using floppies?"

"I don't even have the words to tell you all the things wrong with that," I laughed, shaking my head and holding my face in my hands. "Look, first thing tomorrow, I'm sending a guy down here with a new computer and—"

"Don't bother. I'm all sorted with this one. Plus, you know how I hate handouts."

"It's not a handout," I assured him. "It actually hurts my soul watching you work on this heap of garbage. Seriously, will you please let me buy you a new computer?"

"No."

"Fine. Whatever. I'm doing it anyway. Now come on, let's go get that beer."

I stood back up and kicked a pile of trash out of the way and walked to the door. Looking out over the gym, I watched the raw energy of the kids and stood in awe at their determination, their ambition, their pure hunger to perform at their best. I may have had celebrity clients, but their wealth often meant they thought they were too good to put in the effort. Most of them, including Gigi, thought they just had to turn up and look pretty. These guys, on the other hand, they were working their fists down to the bone.

"They're all real firecrackers, aren't they?" Bob asked as he joined me at my side.

"Absolutely."

"That dude there, Dylan," he said, pointing to the boy in the ring. "I got him pinned down as the next heavyweight champ."

"You really think so?"

"I know so."

We both watched him for a moment. His technique wasn't perfect, and his moves were a little sloppy, but his eyes... They showed his real promise. A fire burned in them. He knew he was going to be the best.

"Hey, boss, where you goin'?" Dylan asked as he saw us walking toward the exit.

"I'll be back soon," Bob called out across the ring.

"I got some new moves to show you!"

"You hang on right there. I'll be back later to see 'em."

As we stepped outside, I couldn't help but envy the bond Bob had with his clients. Except they didn't seem like clients. They were more like family to him. I noticed the way Dylan talked to him, like he was more like his son than some random customer in the gym.

"So, where we headin'?" Bob asked as we walked across the parking lot.

"I was thinkin' that new place on Main Street."

"That fancy as shit new bar? I don't think so. How about Gad's?"

"Gad's? That old dive?"

"Hey, it used to be good enough for you."

I had loved Gad's and spent many an evening screeching my heart out to the karaoke machine while knocking back tequilas. It was the kind of place that still had sawdust on the floor and only a single swinging light bulb above each table.

"You're right. Gad's it is."

Bob looked around for my car then stopped in the middle of the lot when he couldn't find it. "Where's your Mercedes?" he asked, looking puzzled.

"Didn't bring it today. I'm in the Porsche." I pointed toward the blacked-out Cayenne still sparkling from its last valet service.

"Fuck," Bob breathed when he saw it. "When did you get that thing?"

"About six months ago, I think."

"Jesus, I can't keep up with your cars. Seems like you've got a new one every month."

That was only a slight exaggeration. I was a big boy and loved my big boy toys. Besides, what was the point in working hard and earning a fuck-ton of money if I couldn't enjoy myself and spend it on what I liked? Cars were my weakness, and there was little I loved more than getting behind the wheel of a brand new, luxury vehicle.

As we climbed inside, I noticed Bob running his hands over the leather upholstery.

"Nice, right?"

"Gorgeous," he said.

"You know, I could probably get you a new car if you like. Something to replace your truck?"

"Nah, I'm cool. I love my truck."

"I know, but wouldn't you want something newer?"

"She is new! Only got her last year."

"Second hand."

"What is it with you today? Is my stuff not good enough for you or something?"

"Hey, you know that's not what I meant. I'm just trying to help a buddy out. I've got money to spend, so why not spend it on you?"

The energy in the air thickened, and as I drove away, I realized I'd probably hit a nerve with him. "Look, I didn't mean to offend you."

"It's cool. I know you're not a dick."

"Well, that's good to know."

We shared a chuckle as I rounded the corner onto Main Street. A few moments later, we were gliding up outside Gad's.

"Christ, it looks as dingy as it always did."

The same red light that had been there for decades glowed out from the brown stone, except the letter A flickered in and out sporadically.

"Still got sawdust on the floor?" I asked as we stepped onto the street.

"Yup!"

As I approached the door, I could hear the faint sound of blues music filtering out from the jukebox along with the garbled sound of mingled voices. Pushing the door open, I stepped inside and instantly the voices stopped. I stood in the doorway for a second, feeling the burn of dozens of eyes on me.

"Well, if it isn't Mr. Fancy Breeches Matthew Banks," laughed the barmaid.

I was surprised to see the same old girl who'd served my beers years ago. Time hadn't been kind to her, and her face had developed thick lines and a leathery texture. She smiled, revealing yellowing teeth inside lips painted firetruck red.

Gradually, people turned back around and resumed their drinking, and I approached the bar.

"What'll it be?" the barmaid asked.

"Couple of beers."

She grabbed two Budweisers out of the fridge and slid them down toward me.

"Never thought I'd see you in here again," she said with a flirtatious smile and a lick of her lips. "I see your commercials on TV all the time, you know. I'd join one of your gyms myself if I won the lottery."

"Yeah, you keep dreamin', Nancy," Bob laughed as he took the beers and walked over to a nearby table. Behind it, a baseball game was playing, but no one was watching.

I followed him and sat across from him, reaching for my beer and taking a sip.

"Think she's got the hots for you," Bob commented as he sipped his beer.

"I think I'll pass."

"What? You don't like the old hag look?" he scoffed sarcastically. "You're such a snob these days."

"Ha!"

"Anyway, she'd be a damn lot nicer to be with than Olivia, even if she ain't perfect in the looks department."

"That's true." I took a sip of my beer despite the fact it was slightly warm.

"What's that old witch up to these days?" Bob asked.

"What the fuck do I care what she's up to? The bitch cheated on me. I don't give a flying fuck what she gets up to anymore."

"Fucking idiot," Bob sighed as he looked up at the TV. "I can't believe she did that. I mean, did she not realize how good she had it? And with that little runt Simon?"

"Whatever. I don't wanna think about her anymore. We're

done. And as soon as she signs the divorce papers, I won't have to think about her ever again."

"Wait, she hasn't signed the divorce papers yet?"

"Nah. She's giving me a real run around. Just playing games."

"She's pure drama. Don't know what you ever saw in her. I mean, apart from the obvious."

As I thought about it, I tried to remember what I'd found attractive in her in the first place. If I was being honest, I'd have to admit her looks had drawn me in. She was beautiful, all right, but what really hooked me in was her kindness and her compassion toward people. Of course, the second we were married, she dropped the façade, and with each passing year she grew colder and more hardened.

It took a long time for me to realize who the real Olivia was, and when I did it was too late. She had her paws in my bank account and her claws deep into my heart. But I really thought things could work out between us. I longed to have children, and I thought she wanted them too. And I always thought *if I just work harder, she'll be happy and everything will be okay between us.*

But nothing would ever make Olivia happy, not even my vows to love her for all eternity or my never-ending devotion, support, and money.

I'd never forget the day I knew it had ended for good.

I'd been on a business trip to LA when I decided to return home a day early to surprise her with VIP tickets to a concert she wanted to go to. When I pulled up outside the house, I noticed a Mercedes in the driveway that wasn't mine. But thinking it was just a friend's car, I'd happily entered the house expecting to see Olivia where she always was, the sunbed. Or as I called it, the second love of her life.

But as I walked down the hall, I was aware of her giggling coming from upstairs. Slowly, I'd made my way up, listening to her voice as it echoed down the spiral staircase. Call me naive, but it still didn't click that anything was wrong, so I'd lingered outside the door for a second listening.

"Ooooh, Simon," I'd heard her say sensually.

Then a second later I heard a long sigh and a groan.

"Olivia!" I'd raged and burst through the door. I saw the one thing that would cling to my mind like a virus. The one image I would never forget as long as I lived. Lying in the center of our bed was a tiny guy wearing nothing but his socks, his brown suit crumpled on the floor beside an opened condom wrapper. Straddling his hips was Olivia, buck naked and staring at me like a rabbit caught in headlights.

"Matthew!" she'd screamed, scrambling off him. "It's not what it looks like!"

"So you're *not* fucking him in our bed?" I'd instantly seen red and reached for the little prick on the bed. "Who the fuck are you?"

But he was too shocked to answer. The little bastard was half my size, above and below the belt. He cowered beneath me, ready to pass out. Grabbing him by the ankles, I yanked him off the bed and punched him hard in the face. He yelped like a puppy as he hit the floor. Then he fumbled for his clothes and ran full speed out the door Scooby Doo style. I was ready to go after him, but Olivia stood in my way.

"What did you do?" she cried. "You hurt him!"

"What did I do? What the fuck were you doing?"

Her eyes filled with tears and her bottom lip started to quiver. "I'm so sorry. I never thought you'd find out. Can we just forget about it and start again?"

"You've got two hours," I replied. She stared at me, puzzled. "Two hours to pack your shit and get the fuck out of here."

At first, she thought I was joking. She was actually so

stupid she believed I would just forgive her and everything would return to normal.

"You don't mean that, do you?"

I glared at her. "Two hours," I repeated. "You're fucking dead to me."

After that, I'd never laid eyes on her again, and the only contact we'd had was through our lawyers. That suited me fine.

"Forget about her," Bob said, returning me to the present.

"I pretty much already have. Anyway, I'm sick of talking about her."

I looked across the bar at all the colorful faces, some pretty, some weathered, some familiar.

"Anyway," I said, changing the subject. "Becca. Her interview went well."

"She said she was nervous," Bob replied.

"Really? It didn't show. She was impressive," I told him, watching as he smiled proudly. "I gotta say, Bob. You've done a terrific job raising her. Her mom would be proud."

"She gets more and more like her every day," he mused, shaking his head. "So she did good?"

"She did great. Had a lot of ideas about how to expand the company, which I gotta be honest with you, is a first for an interview. Most people come in all meek looking to impress me. But she was just straight 'Listen up, I got all these ideas.'"

"Yeah, she's never been much of a wallflower," he said with a chuckle. "Anyway, you think she'd fit in at your company?"

There was a hopeful look in his eye like he was eager for me to say yes.

"I'm sure she would do great. It's just that..." I took another sip of my beer that was growing warmer by the minute. "She's awesome. Really, she is. But she's fresh out of college. She's full of that youthful optimism we all get when we're young and think we can take over the world."

"You make that sound like that's a bad thing," he said with a frown, swirling the dregs of his beer around the bottom of his bottle.

"It's not a bad thing, but I need someone a bit more experienced."

Bob's gaze dropped to his bottle. I could tell he was disappointed, and I wondered if in some way I had betrayed him. Loads of people would happily give a job to their best pal's kid just because of who they were, but that wasn't my style. Just because she was Bob's daughter didn't mean she could waltz on into my office and get any job she liked. She had to prove herself like everyone else.

"Besides," I continued. "Her ideas are awesome, but I'm not sure if I want to implement them. I'm not sure they're right for Banks Fitness."

Visibly annoyed, Bob slammed down his bottle and stood up. "I'm getting another beer."

"I thought you were just staying for one?"

He said nothing and stalked to the bar. Looking over my shoulder, I saw him chatting with the barmaid.

Are you really being such a dick for not hiring her on the spot? Or are you just doing what's best for business? I wasn't sure of the answer, but Bob was heading my way.

He slid another beer my way, and we sat in silence for a second. I could see from the look in his eyes he was chewing something over in his mind, so I remained quiet as I drank my beer and gave him time to think.

"I get it," he finally said. "She has limited real world experience, but I really think she would be a good fit at your place. And she'd work her ass off too. You know that."

"Yeah, yeah, I know."

"I'm serious. I ain't ever known anyone to work as hard as

her when she wants something. I remember when she was six, it was impossible for her to slam dunk. So you know what she did?"

I shook my head and shrugged.

"Practiced day and night. Literally. I remember hearing the thud of her ball hitting off the garage wall in the middle of the night and going outside to find her in her pajamas throwing the ball like her life depended on it. She's no quitter."

As impressive as that story was, I couldn't exactly hire her based on something cute she did when she was six years old.

"I can tell you're still not convinced," Bob commented. "Look, I can't force you to give her a job, and I know you think I'm biased because I'm her dad, but I promise you, you won't find an employee that works as hard as she does. Plus, with the holidays coming up, you know you'll be getting all those new people wanting gym memberships for their New Year's resolutions. It's a great time to have someone young and vibrant behind the scenes that can help drive new clientele your way."

He had a point there. I looked up at the TV where the baseball game was still playing. But I could feel the heat of Bob's eyes on the side of my head. When I turned to face him, there was a look in his eyes that gave me a rush of warmth. It was the look that showed true belief he felt for his daughter. A look of true unconditional love and support.

If he believed in her this much, then why didn't I?

I could feel myself beginning to crack, and before I knew it, I was letting out a sigh and saying, "Okay fine. I trust you, Bob. I know you wouldn't suggest her if she wasn't up to it. I'll call her and ask her to start tomorrow."

"Aw, man thanks. You won't regret it."

And as he grinned and slapped his hand gratefully into mine, I had the strongest feeling that I wouldn't.

CHAPTER 5

BECCA

Okay, calm down, I told myself. *You can do this. He wouldn't have given you the job if he didn't think you were capable.*

But as much as I tried to relax and think rationally, I couldn't stop the nerves tying a knot inside my stomach.

When I'd received the call from Matthew the night before asking if I could start that morning, it had knocked the breath out of me.

"Tomorrow!" I'd almost yelled into the phone. "Really? That soon?"

"That soon," he replied with his voice full of soothing reassurance. "See you at nine."

Standing in the foyer of his office, I looked up at the clock on the wall. I was half an hour early. *Better to be early than late,* I reasoned and stepped into the elevator. Looking over my appearance in the mirrored wall, I smoothed my skirt and my hair for the tenth time and checked that nothing was stuck between my teeth. The last thing I wanted was to greet him with a smile only to have a piece of kale wedged between my front teeth.

As the doors chimed open and I found myself staring at his assistant behind her desk, I was filled with the realization that this was really happening.

This is it. This is where you work now. You're not a college kid anymore. You're a professional woman.

With a big smile, I walked out of the elevator with as confident a walk as I could manage even though my legs were wobbling.

"Good morning, Sandra!"

"Oh, hello. You're early." She smiled, pleased to see me. "And you remembered my name too. It's not often people do that."

"I'm good with names."

She slid out of her seat and waddled toward me. "Let me show you where your office will be," she grunted as she clutched her belly.

"No, really it's okay. You can just point the way."

"Oof, no. Lord knows I need the exercise. If I sit at that desk all day, I'm gonna swell up like a balloon. Not to mention with Thanksgiving and Christmas coming up, I plan on eating my current weight in mashed potatoes and pie, so I need to move now as much as I can."

I smiled and nodded. "Good idea."

She showed me down the hall past Matthew's office to an innocuous black door. To my surprise, it already had my name on it.

"Got the sign done this morning," Sandra said, following my gaze.

"It looks very official," I squealed, excitement bubbling up.

"Well, it's all yours." She opened the door, switched on the lights and nodded her head inside. "If you need anything, I'll be back at my desk."

I wondered if I should be running around after her. She was ready to pop!

Alone, I stepped into my office and gawped. *Holy shit.*

It wasn't just an office. It was an opulent room with a floor to ceiling window that looked out over the Boston skyline. Everything was new, sleek, and made of glass. My desk, black and curved so it felt like the dashboard of a spaceship, faced the window toward the splendor of the city.

"Like it?" a voice asked from the doorway.

I spun around and saw Matthew leaning against the wall with a cappuccino in his hand and a smile on his face. "I love it," I gushed, drinking in his appearance. There was something so sexy about a strong man in a designer suit, the cut of the fabric clinging so well to his sturdy frame.

"And you're early," he said, taking a sip of coffee before wiping the froth from his top lip.

I would have done anything to lick it off myself.

"I like that," he continued. "Show's enthusiasm. Has Sandra showed you how to log into the system yet?"

"No. I was just about to figure it out myself."

"Here, I'll show you."

Drinking the last of his coffee, he reached into his pocket and pulled out a metal tin of breath mints. Popping one into his mouth, he wandered closer.

"Just relax," he said, gesturing for me to take a seat. "Make yourself at home."

But I was too nervous in his presence to relax. As I sat down in front of him, my foot started bouncing like it was spring-loaded. With a deep breath and all my strength, I held it in place.

"Okay, so it's pretty easy to do," he said, leaning on my desk and switching on the state-of-the-art computer, which loaded up quick as a flash. "I'm sure you'll get the hang of it easily," he said as his fingers fluttered across the keyboard. "If you can get through college, you can figure this out," he laughed and turned to me with a wink.

My stomach did a somersault as I giggled. *Shut up. You sound like a schoolgirl.*

"Okay, so you see this?" he asked, leaning in over me.

I could smell the sweet richness of his cologne mingled with the natural scent of his skin, as well as the jarring sharpness of his breath mint.

"Yep," I replied. "Looks pretty straight forward."

"It is. You just type in your name and then choose your password and..."

He continued to talk, but I didn't hear a word because all I could think was: *This is the closest he's ever been to you. He's so close you can feel the heat off him!*

And as I turned my head slightly, my eyes met his and an electric tension sizzled between us. I could feel my breath catch in my throat and goosebumps rise on my arms.

There's something between us, I thought, a little surprised. *And he can feel it too.*

"So," he breathed, "does that all make sense?"

"It makes perfect sense."

Gradually, he moved closer to me, inch by inch until I could feel his breath tingling on my lips. *Is he going to kiss me?* I could feel my body respond to him and my heart beat faster.

He ran his tongue over his bottom lip before biting it, and I felt myself melt into a puddle as my inner thighs grew moist. I could hear his breath quicken, afraid he might hear my heart as it beat loudly in my ears.

Kiss me, I wanted to tell him. *Take me and spread me out on this desk.*

"So, that's everything you need to know," he said abruptly and straightened. As he pulled himself up to full height, I could see his cheeks were flushed and his eyes couldn't meet mine. "If you need anything else, just ask Sandra."

"Wait..."

But he was already walking out the door.

I sat in my chair, stunned for a second, staring at the screen as though I'd imagined the whole thing.

Did that really just happen? Or am I going nuts? There was something between us. I could feel it and I know he felt it too!

So why was he practically running down the hall?

As I turned to watch him disappear into his own office, I noticed his coffee cup abandoned on the edge of my desk. I reached for it and realized it was still warm.

CHAPTER 6

MATTHEW

"You okay?" Sandra asked as the day came to an end.

I looked up at the clock and saw it was reaching six o'clock already. "I'm fine. Why?"

"You seem a little distracted. I hope it's not because of our new employee."

"Why would I be preoccupied with Becca?"

Sandra gave me a sideways smirk and raised her eyebrows. She knew me too well. Becca was exactly why I had been distracted all day. She'd been in her office less than thirty seconds and I had almost kissed her.

What the hell has got into you? She's your best friend's kid.

But in the moment, when the two of us were crowded around the computer, she didn't feel like the little Becca I had known when she was a kid. She was a grown woman. A woman with curves that made my hands itch just thinking about.

Jesus the way she looked at me could have melted the polar ice caps. And no matter how much I tried to forget about her all day, my mind kept coming back to that moment when she was so close, I could smell the shampoo in her hair and the balm on her lips.

Her lips had looked so soft and plump too. They were shaped like rosebuds and just begging to be kissed.

"I think I'm gonna call it a night," I said to Sandra. "And you should too."

"I've got some paperwork to file."

"Don't be ridiculous. You need to go home."

"Will you stop flapping around me? I'm not gonna spontaneously combust."

"Just promise me you'll go home soon."

"I'll go home when I feel like it."

"Fine." It was useless arguing with her. She had an iron will and wouldn't let me do a single thing for her.

"Stop looking at me like that," she scolded, looking over the top of her glasses.

"Like what?"

"Like I'm gonna break or something. I'm pregnant, not made of glass."

"Hey, I can't help worrying."

"Just go home."

"I'm going! But I'm also gonna call you in an hour to check on you."

"If you must." She sighed with exasperation but winked to ease the tone.

Gathering my things, I stepped into the elevator and noticed my reflection in the mirror.

"You could do with a vacation," I said to myself. "Your tan's fading fast."

As the doors opened, I stepped out into the empty foyer. Everyone had gone home except for the security guard, Jerry, who had just come on for night shift.

"Good evening, sir," he smiled, doffing his cap.

I was about to walk out the main door when I absent-mindedly lifted my arm to check the time.

"Aw, shit!" I said, looking at my bare arm. "I left my watch in the gym."

"Want me to fetch it for you, sir?"

"No, it's okay, Jerry. I'll get it myself."

It was only a short walk to the in-house, employee-only gym facilities down in the basement floor of the building. Set up with the best equipment money could buy, it was built for the most diehard of gym rats.

Back in the elevator, I cursed myself for being so stupid.

"How could you just forget a ten-thousand-dollar Rolex? You must be getting old."

Stepping out into the basement level, I inhaled the scent of the gym that was a long stretch from the stink of Bob's place. Looking through the window, I could see the rooms were almost deserted apart from a few of the company's tech guys hammering the treadmills. I kept telling them to lift more weights, to give cardio a break, but they wouldn't listen to me. I rolled my eyes as I walked past.

"Pump some iron for a change!"

They all laughed but ignored me.

Snaking through the equipment, I found where I'd been practicing my dead lifts earlier in the day. To my relief, I saw the sparkle of the gold strap shimmer beneath the fluorescent lights. I picked my watch from the bench I'd left it on and quickly slipped it onto my wrist.

It wasn't a particularly sentimental piece of jewelry, but I'd bought it for myself as a treat not long after I'd booted out Olivia, and it had become a token of my wealth and freedom. Something to look down at and feel grateful for.

As I turned to leave, I felt my phone buzz inside my pocket. Seeing my old buddy David's number, I felt a smile spread on my face. Since he'd passed the bar at the ripe old age of forty-five and officially become a lawyer, I'd barely seen him.

"Yo, David, how's it going? Still on for drinks tonight?"

"You fucking bet I am. I've had it up to my eyeballs with this case I'm working on. Need to cut loose."

"Awesome. Who else is coming?"

"Just Bob and Jake, I think. A nice quiet little evening with the boys."

"That's just what I need."

I headed for the elevator, barely paying attention to my surroundings until I passed a mirror and realized someone else was in the room apart from me and the tech guys. At first, I caught a hint of blonde hair and the achingly beautiful sight of Lycra yoga pants hugging a tight, curvy body. Then I heard a tiny grunt as a twenty-pound kettle bell was snatched and lifted.

I paused and watched the figure. I wasn't the type of guy to just stand and gape at a woman's body, but even I had to make an exception in this circumstance.

Holy shit!

It was a body even I would have trouble improving. Strong, toned, and curvaceous, it was pure perfection.

Once again, she grunted, squatted, and snatched the kettle bell up to her shoulder, flicking the hair from eyes as she straightened. Only then could I see her face clearly.

Becca? Fuck! She looks like one bad ass motherfucking chick.

I already knew she was an adult and that her days as a little girl were over, but as I watched her move, I was hit by the realization that she was one tough woman. Not a single inch of her contained the kid I used to know. Even the look in her eyes was different.

I was mesmerized by her moves, and the sounds of exertion created a little flutter of excitement in my stomach. Watching her body in the mirror, I saw that her solid abs were covered in sweat and her rounded muscular shoulders glistened.

What I would have done to kiss those shoulders, to drift my fingertips over those washboard abs. What I would give to run my hands down her sweat covered body and feel the heat coming through those tight pants.

To my horror, I began to grow hard and tried my hardest to stifle the overwhelming sense of arousal that invaded my body. But my visual feast was about to come to an end. Sensing she was being stared at, her eyes caught mine in the mirror and she froze.

"Hey, " she said after regaining her composure. "I had no idea you were watching me." She looked less than pleased to see my slack-jawed face.

"I just came down here to grab this," I said, pointing to my watch. 'I accidentally left it earlier."

She narrowed her eyes suspiciously. "Cool. Have a nice night." She stared at me, waiting for me to leave.

"Yeah, you too," I replied, walking away.

But as I reached the door, I couldn't stop myself looking over my shoulder to take one last look. She was still staring in my direction, a little smirk on her lips as she gave me a cheeky wave goodbye. She knew how good she looked and knew the effect she had on me.

Get your head out of your ass! I told myself. *Becca's off limits. You can never look at her like that again!*

∽

"What's up, guys?"

As the last one to show up, I found the boys crammed

around a table close to the stage. Thankfully, we weren't at Gad's again, but a cozy little jazz club where everything from the drinks to the music to the men were all smooth.

"Matthew!" Bob grinned as he looked up and saw me. "You're a bit late to the game."

"Got caught in traffic. It's gridlocked out there."

I slipped off my coat and took a seat just as a pretty young waitress appeared. With big eyes, high cheekbones, and glossy lips, she was obviously attractive, but she couldn't hold a candle to Becca.

There you are, thinking about her again. Get her the fuck out of your head.

"What are you having?" the waitress purred.

"Scotch and soda."

"Coming right up." She smiled and sauntered off with a deliberate sway of her hips.

"Ooo la la!" Jake grinned, slapping his hands together. He'd always had a soft spot for the ladies. Not that they had one for him. If anything, they were repulsed by him. It wasn't that he was unattractive. He was rich, reasonable looking, owned a restaurant, and drove nice cars. He even had a vacation home in California. But he tended to eye girls like they were meat and he hadn't eaten in a week. Even now, he was staring at the waitress' ass as though he was ready to chomp down on it.

"Cut that out," Bob said, looking disgusted. "She's at least half your age."

"Yeah," David chimed in. "How old do you reckon she is? Twenty-three? Something like that?"

"Exactly," Bob agreed. "She's the same age as my Becca, and if I ever caught one of you looking at her like that..." He widened his eyes threateningly and shook a fist playfully.

My stomach flipped and I tried to look the other way.

"How is Becca, anyway?" David asked, turning to me. "She started work today, right?"

"Didn't really see her much," I lied. "I mean, apart from this morning when I logged her onto the system."

"You think she'll do okay?" Bob asked, concern filling his eyes.

"She's a bright girl. I'm sure she'll do fine."

"Yeah, I thought so," Bob said proudly, looking down into his drink with a smile. "She's got a real strong head on her shoulders. And she's sensible too, ambitious, driven. When she puts her mind to something, she'll really do it."

"I can see that," I thought out loud, remembering her strength and determination in the gym. "She's really got her head in the game."

"Oh, yeah definitely," Bob replied, nodding his head. "She has to work at full speed or nothing. She pretty much sailed through college."

"It's crazy, isn't it?" Jake asked as he sipped on his Guinness. "It seems like yesterday she was this little tomboy and now she's this fully-grown woman grabbing life by the balls."

"I know, makes me feel old," Bob mused with a shake of his head. "She's not my baby girl anymore that's for sure. In a couple years, she'll be the same age her mother was when she had her. How crazy is that?"

There was a ripple of surprise around the table.

"Already?" David announced. "Man, I remember when Becca was born!"

"Me too!" I agreed. "Feels like yesterday."

"Time flies," Bob replied. "Nope. Becca's not a baby anymore. Can't help but feel she's getting away from me. You know she's moving into her own apartment soon."

"She is?"

"She spent all last night looking for one."

"Don't look so sad," David said, leaning over to pat Bob on the back. "She'll always be your little princess."

But Bob didn't look convinced. "Nah," he replied. "I think her little princess days are over."

His misery was cut short when the waitress reappeared with my drink. She smiled as she set it down, bending down far enough so we all caught a glimpse of her cleavage.

"Enjoy, Mr. Banks."

"Oooh. She knows who you are," Jake joked from across the table.

"Of course, I do," she replied, straightening. "I've seen your commercials on TV. Say, you wouldn't consider me for one of your ads, would you? I'm fit too." She licked her teeth and raised her shirt up to reveal a trim, muscular, tanned waist.

"Wow!" Jake howled, his eyes almost popping out his head.

"Uh, I'll get back to you," I said, not impressed. She was hot, but she wasn't even close to Becca, and she wasn't anywhere near as charming or cute either. "Thanks for the drink," I said, tipping her twenty dollars. "Have a good night."

She stood next to our table for a second, as though she was waiting for me to fall at her feet. When I didn't, she just stared at the cash, huffed, and walked away.

"She did not like that," Bob observed dryly, watching her storm off. "Although I gotta admit, you were a bit shitty with her."

"I was no such thing," I laughed. "Besides, what did she think I was gonna do? Fawn all over her and cast her in my next commercial just because she flashed some flesh at me?"

"Man, the things I would do to her," Jake groaned, still ogling her from across the room.

"Jake, I think you have a problem," I joked. "You've been single too long."

But he wasn't listening because his attention had been captured by another pretty girl walking across the room, a customer wearing a long red dress.

"Fuck," he said. "Look at that."

"She's not a zoo exhibit," I told him.

"Shameless," Bob jeered. "You should be ashamed of himself. That's someone's daughter."

CHAPTER 7

BECCA

"I'll take it!" I beamed.

"Wow, that was a quick decision," the landlord said.

"Yeah, well I don't like to waste time. It's perfect for me."

I'd spent the last couple days looking for apartments in my budget, and I'd fired off a bunch of emails as well. I needed to get out of my dad's house and into my own place immediately.

Being back at home made me feel like a kid. Not to mention Dad point blank refused to let me watch my favorite reality TV shows or decorate for the holidays the way I wanted. Thanksgiving was just over a week away and then the Christmas season would start. I wanted to be able to deck my halls like Clark Griswold.

This one wasn't the prettiest, but it had everything I needed, was in my price range, and, as far as I could see, had nothing hugely wrong with it. With a few tasteful poster prints on the wall, some trinkets on the surfaces, a shitload of Christmas decorations scattered about, and a few plants, it could look really nice.

"I can sign the lease today," I suggested. "When can I move in?"

"It's empty now, and I suppose there's nothing holding you back from moving in right away." He thought for a second and looked out the window. "Okay, how about you pay the deposit and first month's rent today, and you can move in tonight? How does that sound?"

"Sounds perfect. I'll send you the money now."

Within the hour, the money was in his account, the lease was signed, and I had a very happy landlord. He tossed the keys at me and I caught them with a smile.

"Good night!" He looked pleased as punch as he walked out, closing the door gently behind him.

I was left in an empty apartment, and with only me standing in it, it felt huge and cavernous. Some of the furniture had been left behind from the previous renters, but there was so much left to buy. I couldn't wait to start shopping and filling the place with my own things. Except the boy band posters. They were staying at home.

For a few minutes, I walked from room to room in a state of pure joy.

I have a job. I have my own place. I feel like a proper adult.

Now all there was to do was bring all my stuff from back home, most of which was still packed up from when I left college.

Deciding the only person who could help was my dad, I reached for my phone. When he answered, I could hear cheesy jazz playing over the line along with his dumb friend's stupid voice. Jake was a real jerk, and I never really understood why Dad hung out with him.

"Sweetheart! We were just talking about you," his voice yelled over the music.

"Where are you?"

"Out with the boys! Boys, say hello!" There was a loud

cheer from his friends, and it felt like a tidal wave hitting my ear.

"Who's all there?" I asked.

"Oh, just the usual suspects. David, Jake, and Matthew."

Matthew. My stomach clenched tightly at just the thought of him. The way he'd looked at me earlier in the gym set my insides on fire. It wasn't just lust in his eyes; it was admiration too. He was looking at me, watching my every move as though he was impressed. His gaze said he found me attractive, but at the same time, he didn't regard me as just a piece of ass.

"Matthew's been telling me all about how well you did on your first day."

"Oh?" My cheeks burned at the thought of him talking about me. "So, Dad," I began, changing the subject. "You'll never guess where I'm standing now."

"I dunno. Tell me."

"No, you have to guess."

"I hate it when you do this. I dunno. Are you on top of the Eiffel Tower?"

"I'm in my own apartment!"

There was a scuffling noise as though he'd dropped his phone followed by the sound of him swearing. When he came back on the line, he sounded breathless. "Your own apartment? Becca! How did that happen so fast?"

"It was easy. I saw a place I liked, paid the rent and deposit and bam, got the keys."

"So that's it? You don't live with me no more?"

I sighed silently. "Dad, don't be like that. I'm only a ten-minute drive away."

"Aw, honey, but still. I've loved you being at home so much."

"Well, Thanksgiving is coming up and Christmas is around the corner after that, so I'll be around. And I'll still be home almost every day for one of your magic hot chocolates. Promise."

"You better," he grumbled unhappily. "So, I suppose you want me to lug all your stuff over?"

"If you wouldn't mind."

"Of course not, Princess. Just say when and I'll be there."

I woke up with the sun in my eyes and the sound of birds chirping in my ears. With a big stretch, I sat up and looked around the room at all the boxes and bags Dad had brought the night before. Like the father of the freakin' century, he'd cut short his time at the bar and headed over here, bringing all my things stuffed into the back of his truck.

Of course he did all the usual dad stuff and inspected the walls for dampness, the plumbing for leaks, and the locks for weaknesses. But even he had to admit that I'd done a solid job finding a decent place.

"It's in a good neighborhood too," he'd commented, eventually relaxing. "And you're not far away at all."

"Exactly. I'll be fine here. So you can stop worrying. I'm not a kid anymore."

"I know you're not," he'd agreed a little sullenly. "But once a dad always a dad." He smiled, albeit sadly, giving me a tight hug before leaving me to spend my first night alone. "No big parties!" he said with a wag of his finger as he closed the door.

But a party was the last thing on my mind. After my first day working at Matthew's, I was both exhausted and overcome with the excitement of all the changes in my life.

This time last week I was getting ready to leave New York, and now I was in my own apartment with a new job. And a pretty lucrative one at that. I may have been joining

Matthew's team as a total noob, but he had offered a competitive salary that would allow me to comfortably afford this apartment.

With a yawn, I walked into the bathroom and marveled at the idea of having my own shower.

Ah, my own bathroom. No other student waiting outside or Dad knocking on the door moaning for me to hurry up. It's just me and me alone.

Switching on the taps, I watched the steam drift up from the hot water and fill the room. Stepping into the water, I luxuriated in the heat before soaping myself up. As a treat when I'd left work yesterday, I'd bought myself the fanciest shower gel I could find filled with sumptuous scents of essential oils and flowers.

It was heaven. As I rubbed my naked body, I found my hand drifting down my stomach and lower until it was between my legs.

Whoa, rein yourself in. You've got to hurry and get ready for work. You don't have time for this.

But as much as I tried to control myself, I couldn't stop the urge to indulge that delicious creaminess inside me. It had been building since that tense moment with Matthew in my office. I knew he'd wanted to kiss me as much as I'd wanted to kiss him. I could see it in his eyes, in the way his breath quickened, and how his skin flushed pink. Then there was the way he'd looked at me in the gym, his eyes not missing a single part of my body.

I couldn't stop myself tumbling into a daydream where we were alone in the gym. He'd walk in on me practicing my squats, his eyes scanning my curves.

"That's pretty good form," he'd say as he walked up behind me, placing his hands on my hips and watching me dip down in front of him. "Of course, I could help you improve it. If you just move a little like this, keep your shoulders like this, and suck in your stomach." His hand would linger on my abs, holding me in the correct position.

I grew wetter at the thought of him telling me what to do and analyzing each move of my body beneath my tight clothing.

"It's time for you to stretch," he'd say, and I'd put down my weights to touch my toes. Then I'd sink onto the mat, pulling my thighs apart to perform my favorite move, the side splits.

"Fuck, that's hot," he'd murmur, lowering himself beside me. "You have a perfect body."

He'd run his hands down my leg, admiring my strength before slowly tracing his fingers back up the insides of my thigh, this time teasing me with the promise of going further.

I'd soak right through my yoga pants, showing him how much I wanted him. Only then would he let his fingers drift over my mound, lightly at first, then harder.

Touching myself, I pretended it was his fingers pushing themselves between my lips before slipping inside me.

In my dream he was tore my pants from my body to reveal my wet pussy. Unable to control himself, he'd kneel behind me and lower his face between my legs to suck hungrily. I'd push myself onto his mouth, grinding against his tongue as a hard, fast climax threatened to burst out of me.

"I need to fuck you," he'd grunt, removing his cock from his pants.

"Wait," I'd pant. "You can't yet. I'm a virgin."

But that would only make him hungrier for me.

"I'll be gentle," he'd promise. "At first."

Slowly, he'd push the tip of his cock against me, opening me. His hands would slide around my body, cupping my breasts as he kissed my neck. Then he'd thrust deep inside me, slowly at first then harder as he lost the ability to control himself.

I imagined the noises he'd make as he came, the grunts, the groans, the roar that escaped his mouth as he reached a head-spinning climax.

I imagined his fingers gripping my breasts so hard they'd leave red prints on my skin and the twitch of his cock as he emptied himself deep inside me.

With my fingers rubbing furiously at my clit, I came hard, screaming as I grabbed the shower curtain, my legs trembling and my eyes rolling back in my head. My voice bounced off the tiles as I almost lost my balance, falling against the wall as my entire body shuddered.

Then I was panting as the steam swirled around me, the hot water battering off my still quivering body. *Good Lord...*

CHAPTER 8

MATTHEW

My brand consultant, Coby, was staring at my latest plans and shaking his head.

"You don't like it?" It wasn't much of a question but rather a subtle observation.

"I wouldn't go as far as to say I don't like it exactly, but..." He swept a hand through his green hair and shuffled his oversized sneakers against the carpet. "I can't help but notice your plans are a little too...I dunno, traditional."

"What's wrong with traditional?"

He glanced up from his iPad screen with pure horror on his face. "Okay. In the world of marketing, unless you're selling wallpaper to old ladies, traditional is a bad word."

"It is?"

"Who the hell wants to be traditional in this hyper-capitalist, extra-individualist society where we're all fighting for attention?" he asked rhetorically. "Traditional is about as exciting as roast dinner at your least favorite aunt's. What we want is funky, now, edgy, totally extra, and over the moon."

"Seriously?" I was skeptical.

"Yeah, we really need to get some crunch into your next advertising campaign. You know, more pow for your buck."

"I literally have no idea what you're talking about."

Thankfully Sandra appeared in the doorway to cut our conversation short. "You've got a visitor," she announced, and by the look on her face, it wasn't someone she welcomed.

"Is it Eddie?" I mouthed, trying to be discreet.

"It's worse," she mouthed back.

How the hell could it be worse?

"Coby, is it okay if I leave the designs for the new ad campaign with you? You seem to know what you're talking about."

"Yeah, that's totes rad, man. I'll get some plans drawn up."

"Awesome."

Outside the board room, I followed Sandra and looked down toward the waiting room. "Where are they?"

"*She* just blustered right into your office and made herself comfortable."

"She? Aw, shit is it Gigi?"

"No it's—"

"Matthew! I thought I heard that sexy voice of yours."

A figure stepped into my office doorway clad in a tight, white dress with pearls draped around her neck. Her hair, though still in her signature shade of blonde, was cut shorter with a Jackie O flip at the ends.

"Olivia? What the hell are you doing here?"

"That's no way to greet your wife."

"Ex-wife," I corrected her.

"Not yet," she retorted, holding up one finger.

I looked at Sandra, but she was desperately trying to stay out the conversation, busying herself in her notebook. Hurrying Olivia back inside my office, I closed the door behind me as my blood pressure increased.

"You've got some fucking nerve coming here," I spat.

"I've got nerve? You're the one who had the nerve to try and give me fuck all in the divorce settlement."

"Ah, that's why you're here. Of course," I snarked, sarcasm and disdain dripping from my tongue. "How could I have been so stupid to assume you might have wanted to, I dunno, apologize!"

She let out a dramatic cackle like a witch and took a seat on the couch. Crossing her legs daintily, she put on all the airs and graces she had no doubt obtained from living with Simon.

You look ridiculous, I thought. *You could never be a lady.*

"Why are you here?" I asked, still standing.

"I came to talk."

"There's nothing to talk about," I said. "All I need is for you to sign the papers."

She clasped her hands on her lap, and I noticed her previously sharp as shit red acrylic nails had been replaced with a more tasteful and short style painted a pearly white.

"We broke up," she said, looking into her hands. "Simon and me. I just thought you might want to know."

I paused for a second and eyed the look on her face. She was trying her best to look demure and fragile, but there was no hiding the hawkish fierceness behind her features, or the coldness in her eyes.

"What a coincidence," I commented dryly. "You split up with Simon and here you are."

"It's not like that," she insisted, her head still bowed. She sniffed as though she was trying to force herself to cry, but her eyes remained dry. "What I did with Simon was wrong. I know that now."

"You know that *now*? Wow, it sure as shit took you a while to figure it out."

"Please don't mock me," she said, finally raising her head and tucking her hair behind her ears, which were adorned with small pearls to match her necklace, no doubt gifts from Simon or some other shmuck who fell for her lines.

"You probably think I'm a real stupid bitch, but..."

"That's an understatement," I laughed.

"Will you just listen?" she cried. "Please!"

Her voice was getting on my nerves, and her amateur dramatics were making me cringe.

"I'll admit I made a mistake," she sniffed, her eyes still dry. "But what marriage doesn't go through difficulties now and again?"

"You riding someone else's cock is a little more than a difficulty," I stated, feeling the anger well up inside me.

"Do you have to be so crude?" she feigned embarrassment. "I mean, really..."

I moved toward the door and opened it. Looking out, I saw Sandra sitting at her desk trying her hardest to ignore the unfolding drama.

"What do you want?" I asked Olivia. "Are you here to discuss the settlement? Or to put on the waterworks and pretend you're heartbroken."

She stood up and shimmied over to me without a hint of sadness on her face. Not a single tear had been shed. Her face was perfectly powdered in thick foundation as it had been the second she walked in the door.

"I was thinking maybe you could forgive me?"

I stared at her for a second, confused. She couldn't be serious.

Raising a hand, she rested it gently on my shoulder and squeezed, as though her magic touch was all I needed to fall for her again. When that didn't seem to work, she narrowed her eyes and put on her best sexy face, smiling and cocking her head to the side like a flirtatious nymph.

"Come on, Matthew, it's almost Christmas. What better time for forgiveness? We could try again, couldn't we?" She stepped closer. "I know I did wrong. And I know things weren't perfect between us." She gasped as if an idea had just occurred to her. "We could try for a baby. It's what you always wanted, right? A child to spoil."

I didn't want to react to that, but I couldn't help it. Something twinged at the back of my mind that made me almost consider the idea. I always had wanted a child, and when we'd married, I'd assumed a whole troop of children would soon follow. But they never came. Olivia, despite previously telling me she would love to be a mother, became cold and detached from the idea not long after we wed.

"I'm too young to be a mother," she'd say. "I want to keep my figure and freedom a little while longer."

But soon that little while turned to years, then a decade passed and I'd resigned myself to thinking children weren't in my future.

"We could always adopt," I'd tried to reason, but she didn't like that idea either.

"You won't love them the same way as you'd love your own," she'd told me, although it was insane. "You could pretend, but it just wouldn't feel the same."

"A baby…" I mused, looking into her eyes.

She could see the flicker of optimism on my face and preyed on it. "Yes, a baby. We could have more than one. We could have a whole brood. Isn't that what you always dreamed of?"

"It is, but..."

"But nothing. We could get back together. I haven't signed the divorce papers. We could just take off where we ended. Start fresh."

"We could never do that," I disagreed, removing her hand from my shoulder. "Not after what you did."

"But it was a mistake," she moaned. "And a terrible one at

that. My God, I've stayed awake plenty of nights cursing myself for being so stupid. For being a whore."

I flinched at hearing that word. I'd always hated it. "You're not a whore," I told her, hardening my voice as I continued. "But you are a selfish bitch. And you've got some fucking hubris coming in here thinking you can just win me back with a look and a touch. It's over, Olivia."

"No, you don't mean that. There was so much between us."

"Was. There *was* so much between us, but you destroyed it all. You think we can just get back together and have kids? Are you fucking crazy? Do you think I could ever make love to you again after what I saw you doing with that Simon asshole? You think I could ever get that image out of my fucking head?"

She glanced away, ashamed, but I knew it wasn't because she had cheated. It was because I had caught her, and not only that, but I had caught her in the act with an ugly prick like Simon.

There was a time when just looking at her filled my belly with a fire that made me want to pounce on her, but that fire had long been extinguished. Now when I looked at her, I saw nothing but a sad old liar who had royally fucked up her life and was desperate to retrieve it. I could never touch her again, could never kiss her, let alone see her naked body. She was the ugliest woman alive to me.

"I still think we could work things out," she pushed. "I really do. You'll regret it if you don't."

"The only thing I regret is meeting you," I replied, taking her elbow and guiding her toward the door.

"You don't mean that!" she cried. Her tears were real and streaked a path through her thick foundation down to her chin. "Matthew, please! Don't give up on us like this."

"You gave up on us the second you went to bed with another man. Now get the fuck out."

"No, Matthew."

"Get out."

"Matthew!"

I gently pushed her into the waiting room where Sandra glanced up for a second then furtively stared down at her desk.

"What am I supposed to do?" Olivia sobbed.

"Sign the fucking divorce papers," I yelled and slammed the door in her face.

I leaned against the door, and I could hear the sound of Sandra guiding Olivia to the elevators as her wails grew louder.

She's actually insane, I thought as I sunk down into my seat and held my head in my hands. *She wasn't serious, was she?*

A few minutes later, a knock sounded on the door and Sandra entered. "Wow," she said, stepping in with a scotch in her hand. "That was some scene, huh?"

I took the drink from her and gulped rather than sipped, feeling the calming burn at the back of my throat.

"What did you do with her?" I asked.

"Sent her downstairs. Told Jerry to call her a cab."

"She won't like that. She normally only travels in limos."

Sandra sat across from me and reached a hand across my desk. "Forget about her," she said, patting my arm.

"Believe me. There's nothing I want to do more than forget about Olivia."

CHAPTER 9

BECCA

I could hear a commotion from the end of the hall. Poking my head out of my office, I caught sight of Sandra bundling a shrieking woman into the elevator.

Olivia...What the hell is she doing here?

Something flashed in my head, something I'd never felt before that burned deep inside me and made me feel as though I wanted to grow claws and run screaming at the woman.

Am I jealous?

No. I'm not a jealous person, and I sure as shit don't care about Matthew's cheating ex-wife, so why do I feel like I'm morphing into the Incredible Hulk just at the sight of her?

I also wasn't a nosy person, but I couldn't stop myself creeping out of my office to snoop. I reached the elevator doors just as they were closing.

"He's such a cruel bastard!" Olivia sobbed, her voice traveling all the way down to the ground floor like she was falling down a well.

I looked inside Matthew's office and caught a glimpse of him through his half-shut blinds sitting at his desk with his head in his hands. He looked exasperated, and I had the strongest urge to barge in and wrap my arms around him.

I could make him forget all about that bitch Olivia.

All I wanted to do was comfort him, but before I could make a move, the elevator doors re-opened and out waddled Sandra with a look of exhaustion on her face.

"That woman is a lunatic," she sighed. "If it wasn't for the fact I'm pregnant, she'd drive me to drink."

She entered the small kitchen area at the back of the hall and emerged a moment later with a scotch in her hand.

"For Matthew," she informed me when she noticed me watching her. "Lord knows he'll need it."

As she waltzed into his office and sat down across from him, I continued to watch through the blinds as she soothed him. And I couldn't help but feel the jealousy rise in me again. I wanted to make him feel better. I wanted to be the one he turned to.

The night was falling fast, and although it was barely six, the sky was jet black without a single star glittering through the blackness. With a big yawn and a stretch, I signed off my computer and filed away the last of the spreadsheets I'd been working through.

Time for drinks with Janey, a long, hot bath, and then straight to bed with a rom-com on the TV and some raw chocolate coconut macaroons.

Grabbing my coat and bag, I switched off the light and closed the office door behind me.

"You need a ride home?" Sandra asked from her desk. She was also packing away her things, and I was glad she was heading home at a reasonable time.

"No, I'm okay. Thank you. I should be the one driving you home."

"Nonsense. I haven't lost the ability to drive just because I'm preggers." She hurled her bag over her shoulder and struggled to zip up her coat. "See you bright and early."

"Ever think about taking a day off?" I wondered aloud.

She wrinkled up her face as though I'd insulted her. "No," was her curt reply. "I'd rather die. You have a good night now."

I watched her walk away and felt guilty that she was heading out on her own, but I didn't comment again, afraid she'd bite my head off.

I glanced down at my phone as I walked and saw I had two missed calls from Janey and a text.

Hey, bitch. I'm down at the bar early. And there's karaoke on tonight. Hurry!

I had the worst singing voice in the world, something I was in complete denial about after a couple White Russians. But still, there was little I loved more than karaoke.

I was about to walk to the elevator when I noticed a light shining from behind me. Thinking Matthew had maybe left his light on, I turned around expecting to see his empty office. What I saw instead was him bent over a series of papers on his desk with a serious look of concentration on his face.

Gingerly approaching the door, I knocked gently.

"Come in."

"Hey," I said softly, peering around the door. "You working late?"

"Yeah. Coby gave me a bunch of stuff to look over. All looks like nonsense to me, though."

"Anything I might be able to help with?"

"Maybe. These are his designs for the new ad campaign.

It's supposed to attract a younger clientele, but I don't know. Looks like teenage bullshit to me."

I walked over and looked down at the designs. "Hey, these are great," I commented with a smile. "They'd make me buy a membership."

"They would?" He stared at them, frowning. "You don't think they're a bit, how do I put it, garish and random?"

"Random?"

"Yeah, like the color scheme and the font placement. It looks like Coby threw a bunch of ideas into a washing machine and spat them out through a printer."

"It does look like that," I agreed. "Which is awesome."

"Really?"

"Believe me. They look great."

He nodded and looked down at them, confused.

"It's okay," I assured him. "That Coby kid knows what he's doing."

"I hope he does."

My phone buzzed again inside my purse, and I knew Janey was growing impatient.

"I better go," I said. "Happy hour's calling."

"You have a good night," he said, looking up. His eyes met mine with a look that told me he didn't want me to leave, but he said nothing.

"Good night," I said, closing the door.

I didn't really want to leave either, and as I made my way to the bar, I wished I could have worked late with him. I'd teach him a thing or two about what it meant to be young.

I was sipping on my third White Russian of the night when Janey decided to get up and sing her favorite karaoke classic, 'Girls Just Wanna Have Fun'.

If it was possible, she was a worse singer than I was, not that she cared either. She just wanted to get up and strut her stuff. I watched her climb up on the stage and grab the mic as a group of guys at the front of the stage cheered.

The bar was packed and the heat from the sweaty bodies gyrating to the music was stifling. Sucking on an ice cube from my drink, I tried to cool down, relax, and cheer on Janey. But I was aware of a guy watching me from the shadows in the corner of the room.

Glancing over, I saw a group of men about my age wearing the unofficial uniform of the douchebag; skinny jeans, fake designer sneakers, and tacky, slicked back hair. The bunch looked as though they were trying to audition for a nineties R&B boy band.

I tried to ignore them and focus on Janey, but one guy was intently staring at me. Glancing over again, I made accidental eye contact, and taking this to be some sort of green light, he strutted over.

"Hey, babe."

I ignored him and sipped my drink.

"Hey!" he called over the music. "You having a good night?"

"Yep," I sighed, not making eye contact.

"You here on your own?"

"Here with my best girl."

"So not a boyfriend."

Thinking fast, I looked around the room as though I was looking for someone and said, "Actually, he's in the bathroom. He'll be back in a minute." But I was a terrible liar, and even this dweeb could see through my ruse.

"Oh yeah? Well, he must have been in that bathroom a long time because you've been on your own for a while."

"How would you know? You been stalking me?"

He raised an eyebrow and leaned over my table. Up close,

I could smell his cheap cologne mixed with the scent of his watermelon vape pen.

Ew.

Looking up at the stage, I tried to catch Janey's attention, but she was in her own little world, singing her heart out. It was awesome to get her on her own without Harry in tow, but I couldn't appreciate it with this jerk hanging off my side.

"I ain't stalkin' you, but..." He winked at me.

"Any sentence that starts with 'I ain't stalking you but', is not one I wanna hear the rest of."

He laughed and made some kind of ridiculous twisted expression with his mouth which I could only assume he thought was sexy. "All I'm saying is that I notice a pretty girl when I see one and—"

"Look, I'm not interested," I interrupted before he could get too deep in his line.

"Whoa, no need to be so rude and shit," he said, taking a step back as though I'd just attacked him.

"I'm not being rude. I'm just telling it to you straight. I'm not interested," I said, my voice even and calm. "Now, if you don't mind, I gotta go to the little girl's room."

Sliding off my stool, I strode away toward the bathroom, feeling his angry stare burning through the back of my head.

"Bitch!" he spat after me.

I didn't even bother to turn around. *Asshole,* I thought. *He can throw his little toddler tantrum all he wants. I'm still not interested.*

Inside the bathroom, I set my drink on the counter behind the sink and looked at my face in the mirror. I wasn't much of a makeup wearer, but today I fancied making a little extra effort with my appearance.

Slicking on a little mascara and blush this morning, I thought I looked like hot shit. But now it was beginning to smudge from the heat, and my hair looked as though it had been brushed with a knife and fork.

"Look at the state of you." I laughed at myself as I began rectifying my appearance.

"Hey! Where'd you go?" Janey's voice rang out as she barged through the door. "One second you were watching me sing, then I turned and you'd vanished."

"Sorry, babe. I was getting seriously creeped on."

"Aw, really? It wasn't one of those loser guys in the corner, was it?"

"How'd you guess?"

"They've been staring at us all night."

I huffed and pulled my hair up into a ponytail, looking at Janey in the mirror. "Is it so hard to have a girl's night out without a guy interfering with our good time?"

On cue, Janey's phone began to ring. "It's Harry," she said, pulling it out her purse. "I gotta answer this." She walked toward the back of the room where two girls were applying thick layers of gloss to their lips and gossiping about various guys.

"Aw, I miss you too," I heard Janey say into the phone. "I won't be much later. Just a couple more drinks and... Aw, really? Ah, okay. Okay. I'll be back as soon as I can. I love you so much. Mwah."

She returned with a sorry look on her face.

I stared at her blandly, my lips pursed as I asked, "Let me guess, you gotta head home."

"Harry has a serious case of the sniffles," she said with a sad pout. "And he needs me to pick up some cough medicine on the way home."

"What, now? The fun's just getting started."

"You know what he's like when he's ill."

"Yeah, a big baby."

"Don't be mean," she said. "He has asthma. When he gets

sick, he gets reeeeally sick. Sorry, chick, but I gotta head home."

"It's okay," I sighed, leaning my head against her shoulder as we stared at one another in the mirror. "We can have a proper girl's night out this weekend and get really crazy." She said nothing and avoided my gaze. "What?"

"Nothing," she hedged, but I didn't believe her.

"No, what's wrong? Why do you look so miserable?"

"It's just that me and Harry booked a romantic weekend away in a cabin in the woods. So maybe next weekend?"

I could feel our friendship slipping away from me. I hated to believe that we were really drifting apart?

"Oh," I said. "Well, the weekend after next is Thanksgiving, so I'll be at Dad's. I suppose we can catch up when you get back."

"You're not mad?"

"I'm never mad at you," I promised, pulling her into a hug. "Now let's get you home. Don't want Harry dying from his killer sniffles."

Regretfully, we walked out into the street where the cold wind was picking up and late-night party goers were filling the streets eager for a good time. The air smelled like street food, alcohol, and cigarettes, and there was an ambiance of fun and anticipation of late night debauchery. But sadly, tonight I wouldn't be part of it.

"You wanna share a cab with me?" Janey asked as she thrust her hand out toward a passing taxi.

"Sure."

I reached into my bag for my wallet, but my hand felt nothing but the silk lining at the bottom. "What the fuck?" I gasped.

"What's wrong?"

"I don't have my wallet."

"Shit. Did you leave it in the bar?"

"No, I used cash that was in my pocket for the drinks. Aw, crap I think I left it in my office."

The taxi pulled up beside us and Janey opened the back door. "You coming?"

"Nah, I better head back and get it."

"Are you sure? Couldn't you just get it in the morning?"

"I won't be able to sleep until I know it's there for sure."

"Hey, girls, are you movin' or what?" the cab driver grumbled as he looked over the back of his seat.

"Jesus, I'm coming!" Janey grouched.

"It's okay. Just go," I told her. "I'll get a cab on my own."

"No, don't do that. I can wait for you if you want."

"No, you gotta get back to Harry. Honestly, it's fine."

She climbed in the back and stared up at me with apologetic, puppy dog eyes. "I hate leaving you alone."

"I'll be okay. It's just a two-minute walk back to the office."

"Are we going?" the driver griped impatiently.

"Yes! Fuck's sake!" Janey moaned. "Text me when you're home, okay?"

"I definitely will. Get home safe!" I closed her door and the driver sped off. "Dick," I said to myself as the cab joined the busy nighttime traffic.

Walking back to the office, I couldn't believe how dumb I'd been to forget my wallet.

Your brain's been in your panties recently, I told myself. *If you were thinking less about Matthew, you wouldn't be so forgetful.*

Reaching the entrance to the office, I approached Jerry, the night watchman. "Well, hello, miss. Don't tell me you're one of those late-night workout fanatics."

Suddenly, away from the crowded bar, I was aware of the tipsiness. I'd only had three drinks, but they'd gone right to my head, and I found myself giggling.

"No. I just need to pick something up real quick from my office." I said, skipping past him.

Hurrying across the foyer, I entered the elevator and immediately wondered who the crazy witch in the mirror was. Then I realized I was looking at my exhausted self; hair blown around in the wind and makeup worn away by the long day. Tugging at my hair, I tried to spruce myself up, but it was useless.

Thank God nobody's around to see me like this, I thought as I stepped out and briskly walked to my office. Opening the door, I saw my wallet in the middle of my desk and let out a sigh of relief.

Right, it's finally time for a hot bath and a midnight snack.

But as I turned to leave, I heard the click of Matthew's door, and a second later, he appeared at the end of the hall.

"Becca? I thought you left hours ago."

"I forgot my wallet," I said, holding it up. "I was just leaving."

There was a wry smile on his face, as though he was enjoying what he was seeing.

"What?" I asked.

"Nothing."

"You looked like you were going to laugh at me."

"No, not at all. It's just it's the first time I've seen you not all prim and proper."

"You mean I look a mess."

"I mean you look like you've just finished partying hard. In a good way."

We stared at each another. There was the overwhelming knowledge that it was just the two of us in the office. An energy grew between us, a sense that we were being drawn closer.

"Anyway, what are you doing here?" I asked, trying to take his attention away from me. "You can't still be working."

"Yeah I am."

"Why? "

He looked down at his shoes for a second and said, "I like working. It takes my mind off things."

"Like Olivia?"

Shit, why did you just say that? That's the White Russians talking.

His head had jerked up, a frown marring his handsome face. "Yeah, like Olivia."

"I saw her earlier. Or rather, I heard her. The mad banshee."

He threw back his head and laughed. "That's one way of describing her. But I'm sorry you had to hear that. She made quite a scene."

I felt the jealousy from earlier rise in me once again, but it was stronger, more intense. I knew I should let the subject drop, but fortified by drink, I shamelessly pried.

"What did she want?"

"Ah, you don't really wanna hear about her."

"I do."

"Really?"

"Sure." I shrugged.

He looked up at the clock, then back toward his office. "Why don't we go and grab a coffee? I've not had much of a chance to catch up with you properly since you started here. We've been working like crazy."

"A coffee?"

Say yes. A coffee is exactly what you need. And getting Matthew on his own is exactly what you want!

"A coffee sounds wonderful," I said. "Just let me freshen up first."

CHAPTER 10

MATTHEW

A guy with a public profile like mine wasn't often able to keep secret hangout spots, but I did. The Screaming Beanz Coffee Emporium was an absolute hidden gem in the heart of the city up an alleyway. From the outside, it looked like a garage, but once you entered, you were confronted with a labyrinth of cozy, leather booths and gold tins stacked to the ceiling with every type of coffee imaginable.

It was also a five-minute walk from the office and open until four am, meaning I often visited the little café to do my thinking when I wanted a little sober time to myself.

Never had I wanted to bring anyone here before, until now.

"I'll have a double espresso, please," Becca said to the waiter, a guy that looked as though he hadn't slept in three weeks. "With the Arabica beans."

"Very nice," he said, scribbling her order down. "And you, Mr. Banks?"

"Turkish, please."

"Of course. Back in a jiffy." He didn't so much as walk

away but rather vibrated into the distance until he disappeared behind the counter.

"This place is great," Becca said as she looked around the room. "It looks like a museum."

"It's a pretty sweet place. And there's hardly anybody here at this time of night apart from hard core insomniacs and people cramming for exams."

I looked over at the table across from us and saw four college kids hunched over their laptops typing like their lives depended on it.

"I remember those days," she mused. "Thank God college is over."

"You didn't enjoy college?"

"I loved it, but I felt as though I was being squashed into a mold. I had to follow each professors' syllabus, but none of it really related to the real world, you know. I would have much rather have gained experience on the job rather than in a classroom. I felt like I spent far too long speed-reading textbooks rather than actually doing any real training."

She was fiddling with her hair as though she was self-conscious. Sure, she wasn't as made up as she was first thing that morning, and her hair was a little tousled, but she was more beautiful in this carefree look.

Her cheeks were flushed from the cold and her nose was pink, giving the impression she had just descended from some ski slope and arrived for a much-needed hot beverage.

Between us, a tea light flickered, its glow bouncing off her flawless skin and high cheekbones. Her heart-shaped lips were moist, her eyes dancing in the firelight.

"That's one Turkish and one Arabica," the waiter recounted as he returned with a golden tray. There was much ceremony performed with him setting down tiny cups along with miniature biscuits, little silver spoons, and sugar cubes shaped like crystals. "Enjoy," he said and vibrated away.

Becca took her small espresso cup between her dainty fingers and sniffed. "Fuck, this is strong."

"Too strong?"

"Nope!" And after taking a deep breath, she knocked the whole thing back in one go. "Brrrr!" She shook herself and blinked a few times. "My God I needed that."

"You'll be flitting about like a hummingbird," I laughed.

She looked over her shoulder and caught the waiter's attention. "Another one, please," she called, and he gasped.

"I'm so pleased to meet someone who's a hardcore coffee lover too," I laughed. "And there's not a single shot of pumpkin spice syrup in sight."

"Hey, don't you go insulting my favorite pumpkin spice lattes. They're the fucking bomb diggity."

I laughed again, happy to be in her company. Everything about her was happy and positive, and as I sat across from her, I felt as though I was being imbued with her positive vibes. It was pretty much the complete opposite of being with Olivia.

Olivia may have been beautiful, but when she entered the room it was as though she sucked the light out of it like she was dissolving away happiness.

Becca must have sensed me thinking about her, because she rested her hands on the table and said, "So...Olivia."

"There's really not much to tell. And I'm sure your old man told you everything there is to know."

"He told me she had an affair with her accountant and that he looks like a mole. He told me that she was a real bitch and made you miserable. That he always wondered why you married her."

"Really? He said all that?"

"He did. Said he could tell she was bad news from the start."

"For real? He never mentioned a thing to me."

She shrugged. "He was trying to be a nice, supportive friend, I guess." Her second coffee arrived, which, to my relief, she sipped on slowly, savoring each mouthful. "I hope you don't think he was talking shit behind your back," she continued. "He was just concerned about you."

"I appreciate that."

But I wondered if all my other friends had thought the same thing but said nothing. Would things have worked out differently if they'd voiced their concerns at the start? Or would I have ignored them?

"Enough about Olivia," I said, sipping on my own coffee. I winced at its strength and set it back down. "What about you?"

"What about me?"

"Do you have a boyfriend?"

She had to. She was the kind of girl who must have endless admirers, many a lot younger than me. She could have her pick of any guy.

"No," she replied, running her finger around the lip of her cup. "No boyfriend."

"Really?"

"Uh uh."

"Because..."

"There's no reason. I just don't want one?"

"What about a girlfriend?"

"No girlfriend either," she laughed. "I'm very much free and single. And straight," she added, staring in my eyes.

The tension in my muscles subside at hearing this. "Enjoy your life while you're young," I advised. "You don't want to get chained down to one person and find yourself married before you get to experience the things you want."

She was staring at me strangely, but I couldn't figure out what she was thinking. Regardless, I loved the glint in her eyes. There was a hint of mischief, a sense that she was playing with me.

"You know I've never had a boyfriend," she confessed. "Ever."

"You're seriously telling me you've *never* had a boyfriend," I chuckled. "That's impossible."

"Why? A girl can be happy on her own, you know."

"I don't doubt that for a second, but surely at some point in time there's been some guy that's crossed your path you liked."

"Just one," she confided quietly, glancing away.

"He must be special," I said. "If he's the only one to catch your attention."

"Yeah, he is really special."

"You still hung up on him?"

"More than ever." Her gaze returned to meet mine and the flirtatious glint intensified.

Wait, she's not talking about me, is she? No. She can't be.

"Have you told him how you feel?" I asked, my mouth feeling dry.

"No. Until recently I could never have told him."

"Why?"

"He was a married man."

Below the table, our knees bumped together, but she made no attempt to move her leg from mine. I felt the heat of her skin against mine and the urge to slip a hand beneath the table and run it up her thigh.

"Anyone I know?" I asked, but from the look on her face, I knew exactly who it was.

"I don't need to spell it out, do I?" Nervously, she fiddled with a napkin on the table and looked at her hands. When I didn't say anything, she sighed with exasperation. "Matthew, it's always been you," she said. "I've never wanted anyone else."

I sat across from her, stunned for a second. Although I had thought she might be talking about me, there was still some part of me that couldn't believe it.

"You're playing with me," I scoffed. "You have to be."

With her fingers still tearing at the napkin, she looked up and said, "Cross my heart." Her face was a mixture of excited, mortified, and regretful, a simmering pot of multiple feelings. "I've known you were the one since I was a kid," she said. "Since I was old enough to know what a real man was."

I shook my head, disbelief and hope warring in my head. "Don't say that."

"I mean it," she replied with a hint of defiance in her face. "There's only ever been one guy I've been attracted to, and that's you."

My stomach flipped. From somewhere deep inside me, butterflies began racing. An unexpected excitement coursed through me as an unstoppable smile spread across my face.

"You never let on," I murmured, leaning across the table. "You never said a thing."

"How could I?" she asked excitedly. "You're my dad's best friend. You were married. I was just a kid. To me you were nothing but a fantasy, but I could still never get close to another guy when all I thought about was you."

Her cheeks had turned scarlet, and I reached over the table to touch her face. "Becca..."

I reached even further forward and wrapped my fingers around her jaw. She trembled slightly in my hand as she caught her breath.

Do it, I told myself. *You've wanted to kiss her since she walked into your office last week.*

As I held her, she closed her eyes, and I moved in. I pressed my lips to hers softly, barely believing what I was doing.

I shouldn't be doing this. This is totally forbidden. Bob will kill me if he finds out.

But I couldn't stop the rush of pleasure that flowed through me. The feeling that I was on the cusp of tasting Heaven.

Her kisses were like silk, the slight moan coming from her lips like music. It felt as though our lips had always meant to meet, as though they were destined to lock together.

Instantly, I was flooded with an intense desire that rushed to my groin, and a raging erection pressed up against the inside of my pants.

She pulled away, shock on her features, lust in her eyes. "I've been waiting so long to do that," she gasped.

I watched her for a second, thinking she was the most beautiful woman in the room. The most beautiful woman in any room. I wanted more of her, wanted to explore all the parts of her that were off limits to me but so, so appealing.

"We shouldn't have done that," I breathed. "We can't..."

"But it feels right, doesn't it?"

"Fuck, it feels perfect."

Her hand moved beneath the table and squeezed my knee. My erection hardened even more, and I fought the overwhelming compulsion to leap across the table and grab her.

There was the strongest feeling between us that it was all wrong, that we should remove our hands and pretend the kiss never happened. But at the same time, the more we tried to resist each other, the more we were pulled closer.

She leaned over and tangled her fingers in mine to pull me closer. This time she kissed me, and her lips met mine hungrily, her tongue pushing against mine.

"I don't care how forbidden it is," she murmured between kisses. "I've been waiting too long for this."

Feeling the urgency of her kisses, I cupped her face in my hands and kissed her hard. "Let's get out of here," I said, breathlessly, feeling her hands slide up my thighs.

Fuck, I thought. *I'm gonna explode.*

CHAPTER 11

BECCA

Oh, my God is this really happening? It's what I've wanted for so long and now my dream is coming true. We tumbled through the door to my apartment, unable to keep our hands off each other, kissing so hard it almost hurt. We pushed and pulled at each other's bodies until we collapsed on the living room couch.

I breathed in his scent as I kissed him sensuously, smelled the divine richness of his masculine scent and felt his strong hands on my body. His fingers hooked themselves into my clothes, threatening to rip them to rags.

Between my legs I could feel his hardness press into me, my own flood of liquid passion burning through my panties.

This is wrong, I thought as I opened my legs for him, *but I want it more than anything.*

"Oh, fuck you're so beautiful," he breathed, sitting up for a second to look at my body. He rested his hand on my stomach for a second and felt the rise and fall of my breath. Then he slid his hand in between my breasts, his fingertips reaching for the buttons of my blouse.

He paused for a second, as though he knew he should

restrain his urges, but he couldn't. For a second, he panted, licking his already wet lips as his cock bulged through the front of his pants.

I lifted a hand to his crotch and felt the length of it through his clothes. Inside, I was filled with both fear and desire. What would I do when I first saw it? How was I supposed to touch it? But at the same time, I knew I wanted to take it, wanted to pleasure it and feel it pleasure me.

He groaned as I squeezed it through his pants, and he closed his eyes for a second.

Gradually, he began popping open the buttons of my blouse, one by one, showing inch by inch of flesh until I lay in front of him with my bra exposed. It was the furthest I had ever been with anyone, and I was filled with a sense of pride that I had waited so long. That only Matthew had seen me like this.

My nipples stiffened and were ready to be touched. Slowly, he leaned down and pulled the cups of my lacy bra down to reveal my pale breasts.

"Oh, God," he whispered, his hot breath tingling my nipples.

He caressed them gently at first, then he lowered his mouth and sucked on my nipples, his tongue running circles around each of them in turn. His grip on my breasts hardened as his fingers began to dig into my flesh.

Moving his mouth lower, he kissed the space between my breasts, my ribs, my stomach, the sensitive curve of my hip bone before trailing his tongue even lower.

"Take this off," he ordered, yanking at my skirt.

I did as I was told and unzipped it quickly before tossing it onto the floor. In just my panties, I lay before him feeling exposed but horny as hell. Opening my legs even wider, I revealed the wet patch on my panties, and his eyes widened.

"Oh, fuck," he said, resting his hand on my thigh.

I felt as though I was catching fire, as though if he didn't move his hands those crucial few inches closer to the sweet spot between my legs I would explode. He could sense how much I needed him, could see how aroused I was.

Tracing a line down my inner thigh, he brought his fingers closer to me, then a little closer, almost close enough for me to feel the tips of them graze the sides of my panties. He knew the moment he removed those panties there was no turning back. He knew it was the moment I would give myself to him.

With his eyes meeting mine, he slipped two fingers inside the delicate lace and pulled it to the side to reveal my shining lips. His breathing quickened when he saw me ready for him, pink, shaved, and dripping wet.

Something flashed in his eyes like a primal urge letting itself be known. Something that told me he was no longer going to be a gentleman.

"Sit on my face," he ordered. "Sit on my fucking face right now."

He grabbed my ass and lifted me easily, as though I was nothing more than a rag doll. As he lay down, he pulled me on top of him, pulling my pussy down onto his mouth. In an instant, I could feel his hot, wet mouth encapsulate my clit with pure pleasure, and I let out a scream.

It was nothing how I'd touched myself all those times. It was far more intense. It wasn't a fantasy anymore. It was the real fucking thing.

I could feel my body begin to shake as his tongue ground down on my clit. My juices began to flow freely over his mouth, and he lapped them up thirstily, groaning as I rode his tongue.

"Oh, God!" I screamed, tearing at his hair. Euphoria washed over me in waves as my thighs shook violently. "Fuck!"

He sucked even harder, his hands holding my ass in an iron grip.

"Oh, God, Matthew! Matthew I'm... I'm coming!!"

With a surge of violent shudders, I reached a climax that rocked my body from the inside out and evaporated every single thought in my head until I was nothing but pure pleasure and white heat and ecstasy.

I thought I would never stop shaking. But the feeling melted away and I was left trembling and breathless. He still worked his tongue against me, but it felt so good it hurt, and I pushed his face away.

"Stop," I said, rolling off him and collapsing on the floor. "Oh, my fucking God."

I felt as though I had forgotten most of the words in my head and just stared blankly at the ceiling seeing stars. When I rolled over, I saw him looking at me with pure admiration in his eyes.

"You're quite the screamer," he smirked.

"I've never..." I gasped, still sucking in air. "I mean, I didn't even know I could feel like that."

He lay on the floor beside me and put a hand on my stomach, stroking me gently. My body was limp and overcome with pleasure, but I needed more, and as I pressed myself against his body, I grew wet again.

Rolling on top of him, I straddled his hips. He was still dressed, and there was something so powerful about him being clothed while I was naked. I was vulnerable in his arms.

But I was desperate to see what was beneath his shirt and longed to drag my fingertips over the muscles I had dreamed of for years. Tearing at his shirt, I pulled it from his chest, his muscles bronze and glistening. Scratching my fingernails over him, I watched as goose bumps rose over his skin. He bit his lip as it tickled and wriggled beneath me.

"You can do it harder if you like," he moaned, running his hands up my sides and holding me in place. He pressed his hard cock against me as I scratched him again, this time harder, leaving long, red lines down his chest like claw marks.

Lowering my hands to his stomach, I felt his abs contract beneath my fingertips and marveled in the strength of his body. Then I felt for his belt and pulled it free from his pants.

I knew what was coming, knew I had to do the one thing I had dreamed of for so long but was nervous, even afraid of.

Slowly, I pulled down his pants until I was looking at the bulge of his cock through his boxer shorts. He was enormous, bigger than I knew a cock could be. I stroked him through the fabric of his boxers and felt him twitch.

There's no way that's going to fit inside me, I thought.

I may have been an inexperienced virgin, but even I knew he was big. Sensing my unease, he took my hands in his and looked me dead in the eye.

"Are you okay? You look nervous."

You have to tell him. He has to know you're a virgin. I swallowed my anxiety and held my breath. *What if he thinks you're a little girl? What if he doesn't want you anymore?*

"Becca? What's wrong?"

Looking up, I caught my reflection in the mirror behind the couch and realized just how nervous I looked. "I've never done this before."

He looked confused for a second, then sat up. "You've never..."

"Had sex before."

"You're a virgin?"

At first, he stared at me as though he was waiting for the punch line to a joke. When it didn't come, I could visibly see the moment in his eyes when the penny dropped.

"You said you hadn't had a boyfriend before, but, fuck, I had no idea."

He leaned closer to me and held me tightly to his chest. I reveled in the warmth and protection of his body as he kissed the top of my head, then my cheek.

"You're so perfect," he whispered, stroking the hair from my face. "I wish I had known."

I wrapped my arms around his shoulders and gently held a hand to his strong jaw. "I don't want to be a little girl anymore," I told him. "I want you to make me a woman."

Excitement flashed in his eyes and his grip on me tightened. I lowered my fingers to the waistband of his boxer shorts and pulled them down.

"Have you really never touched a man before?"

"Never."

His excitement grew. "I have a lot to teach you," he said with a smile, running his hand down my body.

I pulled his boxers down further until I could see the angry tip of his cock. It was red and throbbing.

"It doesn't bite," he smiled, pulling his boxers all the way off.

For the first time I was face to face with a cock, and it was so big it reached up past his belly button, rock solid and begging to be sucked. I had never sucked a cock before. But all I knew was that in that moment, I want to suck the life out of him.

Taking it in my hand, it felt so natural to run my hand up and down the length of it. Even more natural to place my lips gently on the tip and flick out my tongue to taste it.

"Hold it with both hands," he instructed me. "Yeah, like that. And twist them a little as you move them. Aw, fuck. Yeah, just like that. Oh God, that's so good. No, don't stop. Keep going. Oh, fuck!"

The sound of his groans made me wetter, and I could feel my pussy respond as it prepared to accommodate him.

I couldn't take anymore. I needed him inside me. Pushing him onto his back, I climbed on top, still pumping my hand up and down his cock. He looked at my naked body with pure desire in his eyes and placed his hands on my breasts as though he was gazing upon a priceless treasure.

Hovering over his cock, I knew I needed to feel it deep inside me, but I also knew it would hurt. But in the moment, I wasn't put off by the pain, I was motivated by it. I needed to feel it so I could break out of my shell and emerge through the pain like a woman.

Looking deep into his eyes, I took him into me, just enough to feel the sting.

"Oh!"

I clenched my eyes shut and lowered even further. I was engulfed with pain but by no means wanted to stop. Lowering myself even further down his length, I felt as though I was being cut in half, but at the same time I was growing wetter, hornier, more desperate to fuck him.

"Are you sure you're alright, Becca?" Matthew asked, concern on his handsome face. "We don't have to do this."

"I'm ok. And I've wanted to do this for most of my life. I'm not stopping now."

Taking a deep breath and biting down on my lip, I eased myself down his entire length, letting out a scream as I reached the bottom. His grip on me tightened as he held my hips in place. I remained still, allowing my body to become accustomed to the large cock.

Soon, the pain subsided, and in its place was the most divine feeling. I cried out, wanting more, and he lifted me up and down, grinding his hips against mine as he thrust inside me slowly.

"Fuck, you're so tight," he grunted, his eyes closing as pleasure washed through him. "So fucking tight."

Instinct took over, and I rode him faster and harder until there was no pain at all, just a deep hunger that urged me to rock back and forth. Soon, I was overcome with pure euphoria that reached through every cell in my body until I felt as though my limbs were filled with nothing but bliss.

But it wasn't just the heat between my legs that made me feel so good. It was the power I had over him, the ability to make him close his eyes and let out a groan with the slightest of moves.

If I twisted one way, he let out one noise, if I moved the other way, he let out another. His eyes were on me as though I was the most spectacular thing he'd ever seen.

I felt like a queen as I fucked him. No, more than that. Like a goddess. I felt as though I had no other purpose than to fuck the life out of him and watch him lose his mind.

Taking his hands in mine, I slid them down to my hips and he gripped me as though he was holding on for his life.

"Fuck me harder," I breathed, and he began to pant, thrusting deep inside me at a frantic pace.

Beads of sweat started to form on his brow as he groaned, gritting his teeth together as a roaring orgasm threatened to take over his body. When it wasn't enough, he pulled me down on top of him, my breasts sticking to the sweat of his chest. He held me so tight it almost hurt, and my lungs struggled to suck in air. But I didn't want him to let go.

I dug my nails into his sides as he pumped into me hard and bit into his shoulder as he hit my g-spot. A muffled scream escaped my mouth as another orgasm tore through me, leaving my thighs shaking uncontrollably as I bit him harder.

"Fuck. Fuck! Fuuuuuck!" he yelled as each and every muscle in his body pulled itself tight.

He began to shake, in his stomach at first, then in his ass and thighs. Then every single part of him was trembling as his hands pulled me even closer to him. I could feel him twitch inside me as he came, could feel our orgasms merge until we were sealed in each other's euphoria.

For a long while, we trembled in each other's arms, struggling to breathe with our limbs tangled together. Exhausted and dazed, we remained entangled and in silence for some time, listening to each other's slowing breaths. When I started to feel my eyelids become heavy, I sat up and looked at the entire length of his body.

He raised his arms behind his head and looked up, a slightly shocked but delirious look on his face. We felt drunk with satisfaction.

I felt as though I'd never be so content again. Although the burn between my legs was now apparent, I enjoyed the sensation, feeling as though through the pain I had earned my stripes. I was a woman now.

"I'm going for a shower," I announced. "Care to join me?"

"I don't think I can move just yet."

I bent down to kiss him, then walked away reluctantly into the bathroom. There was nothing I wanted to do less than leave him, but he'd be there when I returned. Maybe he'd even stay the night and hold me as I slept.

As I entered the warmth of the shower, I couldn't stop smiling. I felt like a whole new person. As though through sex I had discovered the meaning of life.

I want to do that every night of my life, I thought as I quickly washed myself. *And I want to always do it with Matthew.*

In a hurry to return to him, I stepped out of the shower and wrapped myself in a towel. From the living room, I was aware of him walking around. And as I stepped through the door, I was surprised to see him dressed and ready to walk out the door.

"Are you leaving?" I asked, my voice unable to hide the disappointment.

There was a guilty, shifty look in his eyes. He looked toward the door as though he was eager to leave, then he looked at me as though he didn't want to say goodbye.

"I shouldn't have done that," he blurted, his words running together.

"But I wanted to."

"It was wrong."

I walked toward him, my wet hair dripping on the carpet. Laying a hand on his arm, I tried to pull him toward me for a kiss, but he wouldn't budge.

"There was nothing wrong about what we did," I told him.

He pinched the bridge of his nose and sighed before running a hand through his hair. To me, he looked more handsome than ever, but had I lost my appeal to him now that he'd had me?

I started to feel a twinge of anger develop in my gut. Sensing the tension in me, he took my face in his hands and kissed my forehead.

"Becca, listen to me. It's not you. You're beyond incredible. And what we shared..." He paused briefly, shaking his head as if he wasn't sure what had happened was real. "Well, I'll remember that for the rest of my life. You're perfect to me, Becca. But what we just did, it can never happen again."

"But..."

"Your father would never forgive me if he found out. Shit, he's my best friend. He trusts me." He let go of me abruptly and walked to the door. "I'm so sorry," he said, then opened the door and walked out.

As the door closed behind him, I stared at the spot he'd just stood in. A girl weaker than me would have crumbled. Might have even felt as though they'd been used.

But all I could think was that through losing my virginity, I had earned a superpower. I knew how to blow his mind and make him touch Heaven. I had given him the time of his life and he fucking well knew it.

He'll be back, I thought with a smile as I returned to the bathroom. *He won't be able to stop dreaming about me.*

CHAPTER 12

MATTHEW

As I walked out of her apartment and reached the sidewalk, I felt the cold air sting my burning cheeks. Inside my clothes, I was sweating. I could still smell her on me, the scent of her perfume clinging to my skin.

I felt the need to raise my fingers and press them to my lips. The same lips that had brought her to a screaming orgasm.

I couldn't believe what I had done.

When I saw the yellow light of a cab in the distance, I flung out my hand. It came to a screeching halt beside the curb and I climbed in.

"Where to?"

"Heartland Heights," I told the driver.

The man attempted to make small talk, but I tuned him out. It was impossible to think about anything but Becca. But I didn't know what stayed with me the most. The way her voice hit a crescendo as she reached orgasm, the way she made me cum like I'd never cum before, or the look in her eyes when I'd told her it could never happen again.

I felt like an absolute scum bag. Not only had I taken her virginity, but I had probably made her hate me as well.

You're a dick, I told myself. *You took your best friend's daughter's virginity, then walked out like she was nothing more than a one-night stand.*

As we reached Heartland Heights, and I caught a glimpse of the golden gates that bordered my garden. I planned on getting home and doing some serious thinking. I had to truly evaluate who I was as a man.

For starters, I wasn't the sort of guy who slept with girls half his age. Especially not ones I'd watched grow up from a newborn baby. But that's exactly what I'd done. As I tipped the driver and stepped out, I felt like I didn't recognize myself.

"Wow, a hundred dollars," the driver beamed as he looked at the bill in his hand. "Thanks, buddy."

"You're welcome. Have a good night."

Walking up the driveway to my house, I looked around my expansive property and felt horrible. Not because I didn't like it. On the contrary, I had designed the house and the surrounding landscape myself along with the help of a top Boston architecture firm.

I loved everything about my home. But it was meaningless because I had no one to share it with. When I'd first built it, not long after Olivia and I got engaged, I'd planned on filling it with children.

Spanning three floors with twelve bedrooms, I thought it would be filled with all my sons and daughters and their nannies and friends. I thought I'd have all my buddies over every night along with all my family. I thought Olivia might even move in her elderly parents.

But all those plans went to shit. And there I was, walking away from the most perfect woman on Earth to spend the night alone in an empty mansion.

I was filled with regret and guilt. Guilt that I had slept with my best friend's daughter. And regret that I had left her afterward, like she was some cheap mistake.

For a second, I looked into the darkness of the house and considered going back to her. Lord knew I would have loved the feel of her body against mine. But at the same time, I knew I could never hold her again. What we'd just had could never be repeated.

CHAPTER 13

BECCA

I was sitting at the end of the boardroom table with Sandra on one side and Coby on the other. It had been a long and anxious weekend because I hadn't heard from Matthew. But I had chosen not to chase him or contact him either. The last thing I wanted was to look desperate. Even if I wanted to talk to him more than anything.

But as Monday morning rolled around, I knew I had to put my professional hat back on. Any second now, he was going to walk into the room, and I was supposed to greet him as though everything was perfectly normal. As though he hadn't taken my virginity and given me the best orgasms of my entire life.

"So he liked my designs?" Coby asked anxiously.

"Yeah, he thinks they'll be really effective," I said. "And I love them too. I was trying to convince Matthew to pull in a younger clientele, and I think the new campaign will really do that."

Sandra looked at her watch, then at the door. I knew what she was thinking. It was unusual for Matthew to be late for anything. Looking at my phone, I saw it was five past nine, and we'd all been waiting for twenty minutes already.

"Probably stuck in traffic," I said to the room and they both nodded in agreement.

Every second that ticked by reminded me of how nervous I was to see him again. How was I supposed to go back to having a normal boss/employee relationship with him? Was I supposed to stop seeing beyond his suit to the gorgeous naked body beneath?

I'd never be able to look at him again without remembering where his hands had been or what he felt like deep inside me. Would never be able to look at his mouth without remembering the pleasure-filled tremors he'd given me.

When the table grew a little more restless and we thought he'd never turn up, the door opened and in strode Matthew as though everything was fine.

"Good morning," he said, taking a seat at the opposite end of the table. He smiled at both Sandra and Coby. Then his eyes rested on me, a split second of acknowledgment before he moved his gaze elsewhere, but it sent a shock wave through my stomach.

"I trust you all had a good weekend," he said, opening his laptop.

Once again, he looked up, his eyes peering over the top of his screen. His gaze met mine for a fleeting moment, then he glanced away again. But in that passing glance, there was so much raw energy, so much fire. He was trying to play it cool, but I couldn't ignore the way he licked his lips with desire. And at just the sight of him, I couldn't stop the pulsing between my legs.

There was no denying we still wanted each other *badly*.

The tension between us was palpable to the point that even Sandra seemed on edge. She bristled in her seat and said, "You're late, Matthew. That's unlike you."

"Traffic," he said shortly. "It was a bitch this morning."

Once again, he looked up from his laptop to glance at me. Was that a slight quickening of his breath? Did his eyes just linger on my breasts?

Beside me, I could feel Sandra's agitation, and as I looked at her, I saw her eyes tracing a line between Matthew and me then back to Matthew again. She was a shrewd woman and nobody's fool. She knew there was something between us.

"Did you have a good weekend, Matthew?" she asked pointedly.

"Oh, it was nothing special," he replied, but once again his gaze flicked toward me then back to his computer screen.

Sandra narrowed her eyes as she gazed at him, noting his avoidance.

"Anyway," Matthew said. "Let's all turn our attention to Coby's latest designs."

He reached for the projector cable and plugged it into his laptop. A second later, his screen layout was glowing on the screen at the far end of the room. Coby looked on proudly at his designs.

"So, I gotta hand it to you," Matthew said. "I think these are great. I've been advised by Becca that we should move our attention to a different demographic, and I think this is one way of doing just that."

Sandra turned to me, the usual softness in her eyes gone. "So you're in charge of advising Matthew on new demographics now, are you?" she asked caustically.

"No, I'm not. I just suggested some ideas of my own."

"Wow," Sandra replied. "And how long have you been here? A week?"

"Two weeks, actually," I said, trying to keep the edge out of my voice.

"I've been here fifteen years and can't persuade Matthew to change the toilet paper." She sat back in her seat, all of us watching as she crossed her arms over her enormous stomach and huffed. "Sorry," she said, though her tone wasn't at all apologetic. "My hormones are getting to me."

"It's okay." Matthew laughed to ease the tension. "As always, I appreciate your input."

But her mood hadn't lightened. *I thought she liked me,* I thought. *I didn't realize she had a jealous streak in her.* But maybe it was just the hormones. Maybe she was just exhausted from the pregnancy.

Yeah, that's it, I reasoned. *She's just tired.*

Giving her a weak smile to show we were friends, I hoped she'd respond with a sign that all was good between us. But all I got was a chilled stare, her gray eyes like ice chips staring into my soul.

CHAPTER 14

MATTHEW

"Stop it?"

"Stop what?"

"Thinking about her."

"I'm not thinking about anyone," I denied.

Sandra raised her eyebrows and sat across the table from me.

Deciding to grab a quick lunch in between meetings, I'd opted for a light snack in the executive section of the employee canteen. It wasn't a place I often frequented, but I enjoyed the open space, the silence, and the view of the city. Until Sandra had to come over and decide she could see into my head.

"I can tell you're thinking about that Becca," she said, biting into a chicken tender. "It's written all over your face. You look like a teenager with a crush."

"Sandra, where the hell are you getting this from?" I laughed, though even to myself, it sounded forced. "I wasn't thinking about Becca at all."

It was a total lie. I hadn't been able to *stop* thinking about her. Almost an entire week had passed since that magical night in her apartment, but every single second of it was still fresh in my memory. I could still hear her voice in my head and the way she trembled as I kissed her. I could still imagine the feel of her warm body against my hands and the way her skin tasted.

"There you go again," Sandra said, loading up her plate of chicken with an alarming amount of mayonnaise. "You're thinking about her again, aren't you?"

"No."

"Liar. I can see it on your face."

If it was any other employee, I would have fired them on the spot for being a prying pain in the ass. But Sandra? She knew she could be as frank and honest with me as she liked and I would give her a certain amount of leeway.

Still, she was grating on my nerves, and I hoped to God she'd leave me alone for five freakin' minutes.

"What makes you think I've got my mind on Becca?" I asked casually.

"Well, you've been staring at her continuously since she started, for one thing. But you're also distracted, and that's not like you. I can't get a single sentence past you without you staring into space as though you're hallucinating the Virgin Mary or some shit."

She shook her head and shoveled a forkful of chicken into her mouth. "What has that girl got on you, anyway? I mean, apart from the obvious. It's like she's cast a spell on you or something. You've completely changed since she showed up."

"I have not."

Looking up from her plate, a dollop of mayo clinging to her top lip, she nodded. "Uh huh," she said. "You're all happy and shit."

"Hey, I'm always happy."

"Not like this. It's a different happy."

"Oh, forgive me for being happier, for Christ's sake," I laughed, throwing up my hands. "Anyway, tell me what's going on with you," I said, trying to change the subject. I pointed my fork at her belly. "You're almost due. Hasn't your man told you to stay at home yet?"

"Billy doesn't tell me to do shit and you know it," she snapped. "Because he knows who's wearing the pants in our home. Or rather who's wearing the Spanks..."

I was trying to listen to her, but just when I'd stopped thinking about Becca, she strode into the canteen like a summer breeze and lightened up the whole fucking room. With her perfect posture, strong body, and ethereal looks, she captured everybody's attention. Not that she knew it. She was staring at the salad bar completely oblivious to the fact that every man in the room had their tongues hanging out.

A sense of pride swelled up inside me. Only I had ever experienced the pure pleasure of her exquisite body, and that set off some caveman part of my brain that made me feel something I'd never felt before. The need to possess her.

I had no desire to hold her captive, but I was filled with the desire to protect her, to shield her from the whole world. More than anything I wanted to possess that beautiful body and make it reach Heaven over and over and over again. I wanted to look into her eyes as she came and know only I could take her there.

You need to stop thinking about this, I scolded myself. *You can't go there again. She's strictly off limits and you know that.*

But the more I tried to ignore her, the more my eyes were pulled up to her face. Sensing she was being stared at, she glanced up from the salad bar and noticed me. With a wiggle of her feminine fingers, she gave a slight wave and a cute smile. Then she disappeared around the corner and sat out of view.

I stared in the direction she'd walked off in, thinking I was losing my mind.

You're like a kid with a fucking teenage crush. Keep it together. And keep your distance. It's for the best. Just forget about that beautiful body and the way she sounds when she cums. She's just another employee. Just like everybody else.

But as much as I tried to convince myself to think that way, I knew it was impossible.

All week, I had tried to control myself. Had tried to ignore her except for the times we had to discuss business. But those moments were the best I'd had all week. And I began to look forward to them and created reasons out of the blue for the two of us to be in the same meeting together just so I could see her.

I craved her like an addict craved a drug. Needing my fix of her each day to get me through the next few hours. And every moment without her was pure torture.

Not that she felt this craving too. Or if she did, she never showed it.

Throughout the whole week, she had met me with a cool professionalism that bordered on being standoffish. To a stranger, you'd think she almost hated me.

But Sandra had worked it out. She wasn't stupid. She was staring at me now, her plate almost empty. "You weren't listening to a single thing I just said, were you?"

"Sorry, Sandra. I was miles away there."

"Uh huh. Got your brain in your pants again."

"No. And may I remind you that I'm your boss?"

"And may I remind you that employee relations must remain platonic and professional at all times?"

"What's that supposed to mean?"

"You know exactly what that's supposed to mean. You and Becca. It's as obvious as the nose on your face."

"And by the looks of it, you clearly hate my nose."

She mopped up the last of her mayo with the final piece of her chicken. "I don't hate it. I'm just worried."

"Worried? About what?"

"About you." She crossed her cutlery over her plate before reaching for her dessert.

"You have no place worrying about me," I reminded her.

"Oh, really now," she replied, peeling the lid off her vanilla pudding. "I've known you a long time, Matthew. Known the heartbreak you've gone through. I sure as hell don't want to see you go through it again."

Twirling my fork around my zucchini noodles, I knew I had to get a hold of my feelings. This wasn't like me. I was known for being calm and always in control. But right now, I thought both my brain and my cock were ignoring each other. I'd never felt like this with anyone before. Not even Olivia.

"I just want you to be careful," Sandra continued, licking her spoon. "A young girl like that. She's got power over you. And she knows it. Not to mention she's your best friend's daughter. That's a Pandora's Box you don't wanna open."

She was right, of course. I just didn't like it.

You've got to let this go, I told myself, as though it was perfectly possible. *Forget all about her and get your head back in the business.*

The Monday after Thanksgiving, the obscene amount of food I'd eaten at Sandra's that day still felt like it lay in my stomach. She was a phenomenal cook and I hadn't been able to control myself.

I headed down to the gym after work to burn some of the excess calories out of my system. As I pumped as hard as I could on the rowing machine, my head was most definitely not on business. It was very much focused on Becca, who was performing a series of squats and lunges right in front of me.

Why did she have to come to the gym at the same time as me? And why does she have to be squatting in the tightest white yoga pants known to man?

As I watched the bounce of her peachy ass, I couldn't stop the flood of testosterone that headed south.

Down, boy. This is not time to do battle.

But my cock was ready to wield itself like a sword, growing harder the longer I watched her.

She knew I was watching her too, looking at me in the mirror as she squatted lower, then lower, then lower still until I could see the ripe curves of her ass. That primitive part of my brain was rearing its ugly head again, telling me I should run right at her and have my way with her on the floor.

What's happening to you? You're turning into an animal.

I tried to focus on my breathing and the burn of my thighs as I rowed, but nothing could peel my eyes away from her. And when she knelt on all fours across her yoga mat and began to stretch out her back, it was game over.

Right. That's it. I can't take this anymore.

Climbing off the rowing machine, I stood up and walked over. Towering over her kneeling figure, I watched as she moved in and out of the cat and cow poses, her entire body becoming an endless sensual wave of temptation.

"Hey," she said, without looking up.

"Look, I'm gonna come right out with it. What are you doing tonight?"

She stopped stretching and sat up to look at me. "It depends on what your next question is."

"My next question is do you want to go out for dinner?"

"I thought we were supposed to be keeping our distance."

"I thought that too, but..."

There was a teasing glimmer of danger in her eyes, ending my sentence. Slowly, she stood up, drawing herself to full height before pulling her foot behind her butt to stretch out her quads.

"I haven't stopped thinking about you," I said.

She didn't reply and just looked straight ahead at her reflection in the mirror.

"I bet you think I'm a jerk. Just taking off like that and not calling you."

"I do think you're a bit of a jerk," she smirked. "But I get it. What we did..." She shrugged. "Well, it wasn't supposed to happen. We could get in a whole lotta trouble if my dad finds out."

But the look in her eyes was saying she loved trouble.

Setting down her foot, she made a move on her other leg, pulling hard to stretch out the front of her thighs so her chest popped out. My eyes fell to her tanned cleavage and her delicate collarbone.

"So where are you taking me to dinner?" she asked with a cheeky smile.

"There's this nice Italian place near here. Super cozy." She appeared unimpressed. "They do great coffee," I added, and her interest was piqued. "And even better tiramisu."

That seemed to seal the deal. She set her foot down on the ground before lunging to stretch her calves.

"You had me at tiramisu."

I took a step closer to her and could smell the sweat on her skin. There were slight damp patches on her white top, making it almost transparent.

"I look forward to it," she replied with a smile before reaching up on tip toes. Planting a quick kiss on my cheek, she grabbed her things and sauntered off, looking over her shoulder as she reached the door.

"Pick me up at eight," she said, then she was gone and I was left feeling the tingle of her kiss on my cheek.

CHAPTER 15

BECCA

I knew he wouldn't be able to stay away, I thought as I looked in the mirror.

The white yoga pants did it. I'd picked them out especially, and boy did they work better than I could have hoped.

Now, as I glanced over my appearance, I knew I looked hot as hell. The red dress I'd picked out on my way home from work reached up to my neck. It didn't show off my cleavage, neither was it short. But my God was it tight. And as I swayed my hips from side to side, I felt as though I was wriggling around in a giant rubber band.

Leaning closer to the mirror, I checked there were no smudges around my eyes and added one final slick of lip gloss. As I reached for my purse, I heard a car horn blaring from the street. Looking out the window, I saw Matthew's Porsche Cayenne parked out front and butterflies took off in my stomach. I sent him a quick text not to come up, that I'd meet him outside.

As I walked outside, I tried to hide my excitement. *Play it cool. Remind him you are a woman. A sexy, beautiful woman.*

"Hey," I said, climbing in the passenger seat.

His eyes almost bulged out of his head when he saw me. "Whoa, you look incredible," he said, leaning over the console to kiss my cheek.

"Thank you," I replied, wondering if he could see my blush in the dark of the car.

As he pulled away, I relaxed back into the luxury of the seat. I was aware that as we drove, people looked at his car, wondering who the big shot behind the wheel was.

He's mine, I thought as we raced through the city center. *He's my big shot.*

We arrived outside the restaurant, and a valet was immediately on hand to park it.

"Mr. Banks! My favorite customer!" beamed the young man as Matthew stepped onto the sidewalk and handed him the keys.

"Hello, Chad. Thanks for taking care of her." A moment later, Matthew walked around to my side of the car and opened my door.

"Wow, a gentleman," I commented. "No one's ever held a door open for me before. But I've always had the full use of my arms."

Sensing my sarcasm, he said, "Hey, there's nothing wrong with being chivalrous."

Slipping my arm into his, I let him guide me inside the restaurant. He wasn't wrong about it being cozy. Only lit by candles, it was so dark it felt more like I was in someone's bedroom. As we snaked our way through the tables, I looked around at the other diners but could barely make out their faces in the candlelight.

We were seated in a booth at the back of the room, a dark and private table in an already mysteriously dark place.

"Like it?" he asked.

"Definitely," I said, inhaling the garlicky smells all around us as my stomach rumbled.

"Hungry?"

"Always."

"I love a girl with an appetite. Olivia never ate. She was always panicking about her weight." He chuckled. "You know, once, she went for lipo because she'd eaten more than her designated carb count during the week and put on two pounds."

"That's pretty extreme."

He picked up his napkin and placed it over his lap before picking up the wine list. "I'm sorry. We just sat down and I'm babbling about my ex. Forget I mentioned her."

"Already forgotten."

He smiled and relaxed back in his seat. "So, what are your plans for Christmas?" he asked. "It's hard to believe it's right around the corner."

"I know, time really flies. I'm just having dinner with my dad. Nothing fancy. You should come," I said, not sure it was a good idea but not liking the thought of him being alone on the holiday either.

Matthew shook his head. "Thank you but no. I'm not sure being around you and your father is a good idea right now. Besides, I'm looking forward to my day of solitude and the ridiculous amount of food I've ordered for myself."

A waiter appeared out of the darkness as though he'd been summoned from the shadows. "Good evening. Have you had an opportunity to look at our wine list?"

Matthew nodded, turned to me, and raised his eyebrows. "What do you fancy?"

"Bottle of red?" I suggested. "A Bordeaux or a Bergerac?"

His expression said *this girl really knows her shit. She's no silly chick looking for a Smirnoff Ice.*

"We have a Bordeaux Cru Bourgeois," the waiter replied.

"That'll do nicely."

He gave a curt nod and returned to the shadows from which he came.

"Wow, you really know a lot about wine," Matthew said. "I take it you didn't learn it from your dad."

"I studied in France for six months during my last year at college," I explained. "Learned a whole bunch of stuff there."

"You studied in France? I didn't know that. Where were you? Paris?"

"Lyon," I replied. "It's an amazing place. Everyone's so cultured there. I had to learn how to keep up pretty quick. Believe me, there's not a single bottle of Budweiser in that city. And all the kids know their wine."

The waiter returned with a bottle and poured a taster glass for me. I took a sip and nodded, and after pouring us each a glass, he set the bottle on the table graciously. I waited until he disappeared before I turned back to Matthew.

"Have you traveled much?"

"Not as much as I would have liked," he said. "I mean I've been to all the cool spots. The Bahamas, Ibiza, Thailand."

"Aw, so you've been nowhere then," I joked.

"I mean, I've never been anywhere off the tourist trail. I always thought it would be so cool to just take off with nothing except a heartbeat and two feet. You know, just backpack around the world meeting people and living life."

"Sounds wonderful," I mused, and I really meant it. "I mean, apart from the living out of a backpack thing. A shower would be cool now and again."

I looked down at the menu and read the Italian words as my stomach growled with hunger. When the waiter returned for our order, I picked the most carbtastic thing I could find.

"It's cheat night," I said as I stabbed into my lasagna joyously sometime later.

Dinner passed quickly in a haze of wine and chit chat. The food was good and the company even better, and soon giant plates of pasta were polished off, desserts came out, and the bottle of wine was drained.

"I feel so naughty eating this," I said, licking the coffee flavored cream off my spoon.

"You've done a lot naughtier things than eat that," he winked and my stomach flipped.

I watched him lick a blob of ice cream off his spoon, a small smattering of vanilla landing on his top lip. Leaning over, I pressed my finger to his lip before resting it against my tongue to taste it. He laughed and playfully poked his spoon at me, leaving a glob of ice cream on the end of my nose.

"Hey!"

He laughed harder when he saw how annoyed I was, and he dived closer to quickly kiss it off. I was laughing now too as I wiped away the wetness on my nose.

"You're a devil," I chuckled.

Below the table, his hand was making its way up my thigh, slowly, squeeze by squeeze, until I could feel his fingers teasing the hem of my dress.

"I wish we didn't have to hide away like this," he said, looking into his empty wine glass.

"Me either." Looking around the room, I noticed most of the diners had departed. "I didn't realize how late it was," I said, noticing it was almost midnight. "We've been talking for hours."

His hand on my leg told me he wanted me to stay with him for many more, but the look in his eyes was hesitant.

"Come on," he said. "I'll drive you home. Remember, we have a meeting early tomorrow."

Bringing the conversation back to work left me feeling flat and hollow. I'd had such a good night seeing him as not my boss or my dad's best friend, but as a date. After paying the bill and generously tipping the waiter, he helped me into my coat. Slipping his arm around my waist, he guided me outside into the darkness of the empty sidewalk.

For a fleeting second, as we walked to the car, I felt as though we were just a normal couple out for a night on the town. But I knew the feeling would soon come to an end. We could never be a normal couple.

And were we even really a couple at all? Could this go anywhere?

"Thank you," I said as we drove toward my neighborhood. "I had a great night."

"Me too."

He drove slowly, and I hoped it was because he didn't want the evening to come to an end. But eventually, we arrived at my building and he pulled up outside the main entrance. I climbed out of his car and paused for a second with my hand on the door, not sure what to say. All I knew was that the last word I wanted to utter was goodbye.

"Would you like to come upstairs for a drink?" I asked.

He pondered the question for a second and looked up toward my window as though he was imagining us up there. He knew what I wanted, and from the lust in his eyes, I could see he wanted it too. So why was he stalling?

"I'd love to, but..."

He moved around to my side of the car. There was an intensity in his eyes I didn't quite understand, like he was about to say something he knew he'd regret.

"Becca..." he began.

Oh, here we go. It's the we can't see each other thing all over again.

He shifted nervously, taking my hands in his and squeezing them.

"I want to see you again," he said. "But can we take things slow?"

My insides were burning. I wanted him so much, but at

the same time, taking things slow meant he didn't want this to burn out fast. It meant he wanted to stick around.

"We can take things slow," I agreed, resting my hand on his jaw before sliding it down to his chest.

Reaching up, I kissed him gently for a second before brushing my tongue against his. As I pressed myself against his body, I could feel his hardness. Between my thighs, I began to throb with a liquid hunger.

Pulling away, I stroked his cheek. "So I suppose a drink's out of the question?"

He nodded regretfully. "Not tonight."

"I understand," I said, slipping out of his grasp. "Good night."

His eyes lingered on my body for a second, taking in what he was saying goodbye to.

"Good night," he replied. "See you tomorrow."

CHAPTER 16

MATTHEW

I woke up with a raging erection, but I'd gone to bed with one too. I thought I was doing the gentlemanly thing by going home alone last night, but I'd never wanted someone so badly.

The way that red dress clung to her body brought me close to tears. And the way she kissed me as she said goodbye, her breath tasting like red wine and chocolate... I lowered my hand to my groin and sank into a delicious white heat.

"Becca, what are you doing to me?"

I was torn. On one hand I wanted to fuck her freely and often, but on the other, I knew I couldn't, shouldn't be anywhere near her. But it was impossible to stay away.

What the fuck do I do? This is driving me crazy.

If Bob found out about us, he'd kick my ass. But if I couldn't get my hands on her, I'd lose my fucking mind. So what was I supposed to do, lay there and jerk myself off into oblivion?

Throwing back the bed covers, I let the sunshine warm my naked body. Stroking myself, I focused on the head of my cock and instantly felt myself reach the heights of pleasure.

I remembered her kiss, remembered the way her body pressed against mine as her tongue entered my mouth. With my heart beating wildly and my eyes clenched tight, I came hard, ejaculating over my stomach.

When I opened my eyes, the sun was almost blinding, and there were spots of white in my vision. It took a long while for my heart to slow down, and when it did, my conscience dropped along with it.

You're an asshole, I told myself. *You know who she is, your best friend's fucking daughter. You'll go to hell for this.*

Climbing out of bed, I walked into the bathroom and set the shower to ice cold. Then I stepped inside and tried to shock my frustration out of my body.

When I came out shivering, I looked at the clock. In half an hour's time, I'd be back in the office. And back with Becca.

∽

As I drove into the city toward my office, I thought of her. Not just all the things I found attractive about her, but what I had to do to keep a level head in her company.

I was grateful I'd told her to cool off last night, and I was glad she was a mature woman. She took the news well and seemed to agree that taking things slow was a good idea.

Still, as my mind zoned in and out as I drove, I couldn't stop thinking about where this was going. It felt wrong but it felt right. I knew it was forbidden, but at the same time I hadn't felt this alive in years.

Arriving at the office a little earlier than expected, I said hello to Sandra and looked down the hall to Becca's office. Her door was closed, so I slipped into my own office. With a few minutes to spare before our first meeting, I took the time to check my emails. I leaned back with a yawn and scanned my eyes over the page.

Junk mail. More junk mail. A tacky chain joke email from Jake. Who the hell even still sends those? Something that looked like an invoice and some more designs from Coby. But in among the usual names and subject headings, something caught my eye.

"What's this?"

I leaned close as though if I got closer to the screen, I could work it out faster. The email address was just a jumble of letters and numbers at a Hotmail account, but that wasn't what stood out the most. What grabbed my attention were the four words typed threateningly in all caps along the subject bar.

SHE'S HALF YOUR AGE

"What the fuck?"

At first, I assumed it had to be a virus, but it couldn't be. With bated breath, I opened the email, not knowing what I'd find. What I definitely hadn't anticipated was a series of pictures attached to the blank email.

I opened the first one, confused as hell.

Holy fuck. The picture was almost too dark and blurry to make out, but there was no mistaking the two figures in the center of the image. It looked as though it had been taken from the inside of a car staring out toward Becca's apartment. Through the blackness, her red dress burned brightly as I held her.

Who the fuck took this?

I clicked on the next image, then the next and the next. All of them showed the two of us outside her apartment in each other's arms. In one, her hand lay on my cheek lovingly as she looked into my face. In another, I was running my hands down her arms.

Okay, relax. This doesn't really show anything. If anybody sees these, I can just say I drove her home after work. It's not as if we're really doing anything but hugging?

But then I clicked on the last image and my stomach almost bottomed out. Clearer than all the others, this image sharply showed a closeup of our faces, our lips pressed together.

"Shit!"

There was no denying it. Someone knew about us.

Who could have known we were together last night and why did they care?

"Fuck!"

I slid backward away from my desk as though just being near my computer was enough to infect me with the scandalous photos. Then I stood up and walked over to the window.

What bastard did this?

I didn't know what feeling overwhelmed me the most. Anger that someone dared to follow me and anonymously threaten me with these photos. Or shame that I had been photographed kissing a girl young enough to be my daughter.

I had known guys my age who had deliberately sought out young girls for their youth and looks and lavished them with cash and gifts. They had loved the image of being a sugar daddy and having some hot young thing on their arm. But their behavior always disgusted me. I wasn't like them. Or so I thought...

But if anybody saw the photos, they'd no doubt think I was some creep. Just another rich guy on a power trip preying on a girl far too young for him. I felt ashamed of myself. Not just because I looked like an asshole, but because Bob might see the photos, and when he did, I knew our friendship would be over.

I'm such a selfish dick, I thought to myself as I looked out the window across the city. *I can't keep doing this. This needs to end right now.*

No matter how much I liked spending time with her, and how much I was attracted to her, for now she would have to be nothing but a fantasy. As soon as our meeting ended, I would tell it to her straight. Whatever we had, no matter how fun it was, had to end today.

You gotta do it, I told myself. *Do it for Bob. Do it because it's the right thing.* I gave myself an affirmative nod as I reached the decision.

As I turned around to gather my things for the meeting, a knock sounded and Sandra entered the room with a large coffee.

"I took the liberty of putting in two extra shots of espresso," she said as she handed it to me. "You look a little stressed this morning. Thought you could do with the boost."

"You've no idea how much I need it," I said, taking it from her. "Is everything set up for the meeting?"

"Yep! Becca's good to go."

CHAPTER 17

BECCA

What does that look in his eye mean? I wondered as he brought the meeting to a close.

For the last hour he had listened to my suggestions and questions coolly, answering them furtively. But there was no hint of the spark between us that was alive before.

As everybody began filtering out the room, I wasn't sure if I should hang back or not. Deciding I didn't want to look as though I was desperate for his attention, I joined everybody else and walked toward the door. But before I could reach it, I heard his voice from the back of the room.

"Becca? Can I have a word with you in your office?"

I looked back as he packed his notepad and laptop. There was an expectant, though hesitant look on his face.

"Sure," I said, waiting for him.

He said nothing as we left the room, only opening his mouth as soon as we were in the privacy of my office with the door closed.

"Becca..." he began. His face was tense with stress and a line was forming across his forehead.

"Is something wrong?" I asked, worried.

"Someone knows about us."

The words hung in the air for a moment as I processed them. My brow furrowed in confusion. "Who?"

"I don't know," he replied. "But someone followed us."

"Followed us? When?"

"Last night." He pulled out his phone and opened an email before flashing a series of images in my face.

"Oh, my God. Who took those?"

"I'm going to find out," he said.

"What did they want?"

"Nothing yet," he said. "All I know is that they followed us and took these photos."

"Are they trying to blackmail you?"

"Most likely, yes."

I sunk into my seat and looked up at him. The look on his face was making me nervous. He wasn't the type of guy to get stressed out by anything, but this really seemed to have rattled him.

Pulling up a second chair, he took a seat beside me and leaned forward. I reached my hands out toward him, but he wouldn't take them, preferring to keep his distance from me.

"Listen, this is all wrong," he said.

"I know. It's fucked up. Who would follow us? "

"It's not just the photos, Becca."

That strained look returned to his face. Once again, I reached for his hand, but he slid away from me.

"It's us too," he continued. *"We're* wrong. I should've listened to my gut from the get-go."

"But last night was amazing," I countered. "I thought we agreed to take things slow."

"I thought so too, but, Christ, I feel like such a dick."

"What are you trying to say Matthew?"

"That we need to end this," he said bluntly. "If your dad

sees these photos, if he finds out about us, he'll know I betrayed him."

"Forget about my dad. I'm an adult! I don't have to keep answering to him."

"Maybe not, but I do. I owe him that after nearly thirty damn years of friendship. Not to mention, you're half my age, Becca. You're practically still a kid."

"I'm twenty fucking three," I reminded him hotly. "I'm not a child."

"I know, but we can't do this. We just can't. I'm sorry."

He rose out his seat and aimed for the door, but I lay my hand on his arm, and he paused, looking down at it.

"What are you so afraid of?" I asked. "Do you care what people will think?"

"Of course I do. But it's not just that. I feel like some dirty old bastard taking advantage of a young girl."

I stood up and drifted my hand down his arm. I wasn't going to let him slip away so easily. Taking his hand, I squeezed it, massaging his palm with my thumb.

"Fuck what everybody thinks," I purred, stepping closer. "What does it matter?"

"I have a professional reputation to uphold. I can't afford for anyone to think there is any impropriety happening. It could negatively affect my business."

"No one is going to think you're doing anything wrong. You have a great reputation in the business scene. Not to mention, you didn't initiate this. I did." I took another step closer, my breasts pushing into his chest. "You're not taking advantage of me," I said, softly, moving my other hand inside his blazer to stroke his side. "I've always known who's in charge.'

"And who's that?" he asked, the tension dissolving on his face before something twitched at the corners of his mouth.

"Me."

Reaching up, I kissed him as softly as possible. Nothing but a tease of what he would be missing out on if he walked away. Then I took my hands off his body and stepped away.

The energy between us grew, a gulf of heat and angst building up between us. His eyes told me he wanted to take me, to fuck the life out of me. But his body remained hesitant, keeping that safe distance between us.

I could see the desire in him growing. Could see that he was struggling to hold back. Looking down at his pants, I saw he was hard, his cock bulging down the length of his thigh.

"I suppose it's goodbye then," I said, turning around and pretending to resume my work. "If you want to keep our relationship professional, then that's your decision."

I was playing with him, of course, knowing full well that was the last thing he wanted to do.

Then I felt it. The energy between us reaching a crescendo. A sense that he was going to lunge right at me. From behind, I heard the door to my office lock and the slight creak of the floor as he moved.

Any second now and he won't be able to control himself. He just needs a push over the edge.

All it took was a look. And as I glanced over my shoulder and bit my lip, I could see him teeter over that precipice.

He moved like lightning, his heavy body landing on me with such force it knocked the air out of me. With a vice like grip, his arms clamped around my waist as his cock pressed into my ass.

"Becca, what the hell have you done to me?" he whispered in my ear as he took my wrists and pulled them behind my back.

My panties were flooded in an instant. I loved the feel of his strong body taking control of me. I pushed myself against him, submitting my body to him.

With one hand holding my thin wrists together, his other hand slid up the length of my thigh, under my skirt, and into my panties. He tore at them impatiently, stinging the skin of my thighs as he yanked them to the side.

My pussy was so wet it ached for him. I closed my eyes and waited for him, bit my lip and knew he wouldn't be gentle.

He grunted as he thrust into me roughly, sliding one hand around to my front and up to my breast. Squeezing it hard, he kissed my neck as though he was trying to devour me. He delivered great long flicks of his tongue before biting the soft skin of my throat as though he was claiming me. It wasn't hard enough to hurt, carrying just enough force to let me know who the boss was really.

Thrusting harder, he drove his cock deep inside me. I bit my lip to keep from screaming. Knowing that people were right outside my door and might hear us fucking like animals was enough to ratchet the pleasure up to near unbearable levels.

"Harder," I said through gritted teeth.

He wasted no time giving me what I wanted. He bent me completely over my desk and pushed himself even deeper inside me. I let out an involuntary moan, and he clapped a hand over my mouth, admonishing me to be quiet.

I slammed myself backward into his hips, desperate to feel his whole length. Slowly, he lowered his hand from my mouth, his palm coming away wet with my breath. He slid it down my body then rested it over my stomach for a second, as though he was imagining his cock buried inside me. Then he moved his fingers lower, gently placing them over my clit.

"Promise you won't make a sound," he whispered in my ear as he continued to fuck me, the only noise between our bodies the smacking sound of our skin meeting with each thrust.

"I promise," I breathed.

It took all the strength in the world not to scream when he began to rub my clit in slow, sensuous circles that soon turned into frantic strokes as he massaged me harder until my legs gave way beneath me. I buckled at the knees as I shuddered, my whole body going limp from the waist down. My breath came in short gasps as my muscles spasmed, the pleasure so bright I thought I'd go blind.

"You like that?" he whispered in my ear, pressing himself against my back.

"Oh God yes."

"You want more?"

I didn't know if my body could handle it, but I wanted all he could give me. "Yes."

He paused for a second, enticing me, making me even more desperate. I looked over my shoulder and met his eyes, which sparkled with the lustful delight that came from teasing me. He stroked the side of my face so gently it was barely a touch at all. Pressing his lips to my temple, he kissed me softly and lovingly.

"Please, just fuck me," I begged in a whisper.

He tucked my hair behind my ear and kissed me again. There was a look in his eyes that said *don't tell me what to do. I'm the boss here.* I stared at him for what felt like an eternity, willing him to enter me. My pussy was swollen and dripping as I reached an almost physical pain of arousal.

"You're torturing me," I whimpered, but that only made the look on his face intensify.

"Are you sure you want me to fuck you harder?" he murmured in my ear, his breath like a shock wave of electricity that traveled down my neck. I silently nodded. "Then that's what you're gonna get."

He waited for another second, just long enough to make me feel as though my pussy was catching fire. Then he thrust into me as fast and hard as his body would allow him. I was instantly engulfed in a whirlwind of pleasure that forced me to bite down on my lip with such force I was sure it would bleed. My already weak legs became numb, my knees doing nothing to hold the weight of my shaking body.

"I'm gonna make you come," he groaned in my ear as he rubbed my clit. "I'm gonna make you come so fucking hard."

All it took was for me to hear those words and I was toppling over the precipice of control. A thundering orgasm raged through me as my pussy throbbed and contracted around his cock. I wanted to thrash and scream, but he was still holding my wrists behind my back, still imploring me with his eyes to hold my silence.

All I could do was let out a weak whimper as I violently shook against him.

"Fuuuuuck," he uttered in a low rumble as he gripped my wrists hard enough to leave marks. "Oh, God what are you doing to me? I'm...Oh fuck, I'm..."

His hips shuddered as he came deep inside me, his mouth pressed against my neck as his cock twitched as it filled me with his seed.

From down the hall, I could hear Sandra talking to someone, but I didn't want to think about her. Didn't want to think about anyone or anything outside of this moment. I felt as though I didn't even belong in this world anymore. As though my body and the pleasure that filled it now inhabited some other plane of existence.

But I knew the moment had to come to an end, and with great reluctance, he slid out of me and pushed himself back into his boxer shorts.

At last, with his grip released on my wrists, I lowered my arms and turned around as blood flowed back into my hands. Lowering my skirt, I looked down and saw my knees tremble as the evidence of what we'd just done trickled down my legs.

Outside, Sandra's voice grew louder, and we looked at each other in a panic.

"Matthew? Are you in there?" she called out as she knocked on the locked door.

He quickly zipped up his pants and I hurried to return to my seat, turning to my computer screen. He reached over and unlocked the door, and she waltzed in immediately.

"Oh, hey Matthew," Sandra said. "I've been looking for you. I have the files from accounting."

"Okay, great. I'll have a look in a second," Matthew replied.

The atmosphere in the air tightened, as though our secret was ready to be burst wide open. I worried my face would give me away, so I steadfastly stared at my computer screen. Out of the corner of my eye, I saw Sandra look suspiciously from me to Matthew, then back to me again.

"Right. Well, I'll let you get back to whatever you're doing." She closed the door and we both let out a sigh of relief.

"Fuck, that was close," I said. "Ten seconds earlier and..." I cringed at the thought.

"That could have been a disaster," he agreed.

"But it wasn't."

"No, it wasn't. It was fucking incredible. *You're* incredible Becca." He bent down to stroke my hair and kiss my forehead.

"Still feel like a creep?" I joked.

"A little." He edged toward the door, not wanting to leave but knowing that staying would only rouse more suspicion.

"I don't want to go, but I..."

"Gotta get back to work. I know."

He smiled and turned the door handle.

"Wait. Your fly's undone."

"Shit. Did Sandra see?"

"Let's hope not."

He zipped it up with a guilty smile and kissed me once before leaving. As I heard the door click shut behind him, I relaxed back in my chair and took a deep breath. *That was the greatest experience of my life,* I thought. *I want more.* I would have rushed out of my office and right into Matthew's for round two if I could have.

"Get a grip of yourself and get back to work," I said out loud.

Not that it was that easy. As I loaded up my files and tried to focus on work, nothing I looked at made sense and memories of Matthew and what he could do to my body kept popping into my thoughts.

This is useless, I thought as I decided to take a coffee break. *I'm going insane. Like my brain is incapable of thinking of anything but him.*

Exiting my office, I walked down to the little kitchen at the end of the hall and flipped on the coffee machine.

"Having a good day?" Sandra's sour voice asked.

"Oh, hey, Sandra. How's it goin?"

"Great," she replied, but her eyes didn't agree with the word, nor did her tone. "Just the usual. Busy, busy, busy."

"Yeah, me too."

"I can see that." There was no hiding the coldness in her voice or the suspicion in her eyes.

Shit. She knows. She has to. Then another thought entered my mind. *It was you who followed us! You who took those photos. Who else could it be?*

We stood for an excruciatingly awkward moment and stared at one another. Beside me, the coffee machine bubbled and spat as the room filled with the smell of espresso. When my cup was full, I grabbed it and headed for the door as quickly as possible.

"Gotta get back to my office," I announced without stopping.

She narrowed her eyes at me and nodded. "Yeah, catch you later," she sneered.

CHAPTER 18

MATTHEW

What the fuck have I done?
Back at my desk, I felt as though I had plummeted back to reality.
You were supposed to break it off with her, you idiot. You literally did the fucking opposite of what you walked in there to do!
I couldn't believe I'd been so weak, or so stupid. I behaved like a brainless caveman thinking with his cock.
Okay, now you have to break it off, I thought to myself. *Except you just had the best fuck of your life with her. Dump her now and you'll look like a royal asshole.*
I didn't know what to do. I prided myself on being a smart man, a good man. But since Becca had walked back into my life, I'd become a primitive being, ruled by my dick. But as much as I wanted to forget about seeing her, I knew it was impossible to get her out my head. As I sat there, balls aching from the orgasm of a lifetime, I still wanted more and had to stop myself from marching back to her office to fuck her again.
She's got her claws in you, I thought. *She got into your head. Into your fucking soul.*

But it wasn't just her incredible looks that drove me wild, although they obviously played a part. It was the look in her eyes when she wanted me, the way she twisted the power from her to me then back to her again. It was her ambition and intelligence and the way she reached out and grabbed what she wanted.

"Fuck me," I heard her voice say in my head.

I had heard girls say it a hundred times before, but their voices were as hollow and devoid of genuine lust as the porn stars they emulated. When she said it, I could feel her need for me. Truly know that she craved my cock as much as she craved air.

"Get back to work," I told myself. "You have a business to run."

But as I looked at my computer screen, I saw nothing. My head was filled with her and nothing else.

"I'm losing my fucking mind," I said out loud. Turning off my computer, I gave up trying to concentrate on the files I was supposed to be reading.

A drink is what you need. Something stiff and strong and full of ice will clear your head.

I was sitting in a back booth of the Riley Lounge on Duke Street sipping on a scotch and listening to a single jazz clarinet player on the stage. He was blowing into the thing as though he was pouring his heart into it, his cheeks bright red like shiny apples stuck to his face. My mind still hadn't settled, but at least I wasn't just down the hall from her. As I drank, I heard a voice I instantly recognized.

"Matthew? What are you doing here?"

I saw David standing with a vodka and tonic in his hand, the auburn glow of the art deco chandelier casting a halo around his head. At his side was his vintage leather briefcase, a gift from his mother when he'd passed the bar.

"Hey, aren't you supposed to be in court today?"

"Aren't you supposed to be at work? It's not like you to be drinking alone in the middle of the day."

He took the seat beside me and looked up at the stage. The clarinetist had been joined by a singer who purred and shimmied around the stage in slow motion. She was singing a song about young love driving a kid crazy. It could have been written about me. Except I was no kid.

"Taking a time out," I told David. "Needed some time to think."

"Got a lot on your plate at the office?"

I took a sip of my drink and said, "Actually, it's woman trouble."

"Woman trouble? For the love of fuck, tell me it's not Olivia."

"Oh fuck no. That crazy bitch is long gone."

"So who is it?"

"Ah, nobody you know."

He sipped his vodka and winced, then moved his eyes back to the singer as she swayed her hips. She was caressing the mic stand as though it was her lover, her lips making love to the microphone. She was an attractive woman with great, swinging curves, a sculpted face, and raven black hair draped around her cheekbones.

She was the type of woman the rational side of my brain was telling me to be attracted to. Someone mature and worldly. But of course the rational side of my brain had withered and died at the sight of Becca.

"She's a real looker, isn't she?" David asked, nodding toward the singer.

"Meh." I shrugged.

"Meh? Man, you really do have your head up your ass. Whoever this woman is must be really special."

"She is."

"So who is she?"

"Like I said, no one you know."

He sipped his drink and gave me a wary sideways glance. "If she's so special, how come you haven't told us about her?" he asked, tinkling the ice around the bottom of his glass.

I shrugged. "It's complicated."

"Shit. It's not your assistant, Sandra, is it? Wait, please tell me that baby isn't yours."

"Whoa, calm down. It's not Sandra. Unlike my ex, I don't fuck married people."

"So who is it?"

I chuckled mirthlessly. "Jesus, you're really not letting this go, are you?"

"Nope. I'm a prosecutor, remember? Gotta have all the details. All the incriminating evidence."

"What, am I on trial here or something?"

He laughed and swallowed the last of his drink before signaling the waitress to bring another. "I'm just confused," he said. "How long have we known each other? Like twenty years?"

"Twenty-two."

"Wow, you have a good memory. So yeah, twenty-two years. And you've told me about all the other women."

"You make it sound like there was a long line of them."

"I'm just saying it's weird. And it's not like you to keep stuff from your buddies. Afraid we'll steal her?"

I cringed at the thought. "No, nothing like that."

"So, tell me who she is."

"No."

"Aw, come on!"

"No way. A gentleman is allowed to keep his secrets." But the way I acted toward her was anything but gentlemanly.

"So, you're really not gonna tell me, huh? Fine." He was pretending to joke, but I could see he was mildly annoyed. "Anyway," he continued as the waitress appeared with his second drink. "You seen Bob recently?"

"Not in the last few days. Why?"

"Ah, no reason. It's just that he's really happy about Becca working for you. Won't stop yappin' on about it. Thinks it's the best thing on Earth since sliced bread."

I was instantly gripped with a nauseating guilt, and as he continued, the urge to vomit pressed against the back of my throat.

"He worries about Becca, you know? She's not a little girl anymore, but she'll always be his princess. Swear to God she's still five years old in his head."

My gut plummeted. I didn't even know it was possible to feel so ashamed.

"He says he trusts you," David added, and I wondered if he knew what was going on and was thrusting the knife in on purpose.

"Trusts me?"

"Yeah, like he's happy she's got you for a boss instead of some sleazebag. He knows how pretty he is. Knows that guys are always getting an eyeful of her. But not you, you know. He feels safe with her around you."

My cheeks burned as I looked down into my scotch. Suddenly, it didn't seem so appetizing anymore, and I had no interest in hanging around. Like the shady, guilty bastard that I was, I wanted to slither out of the room and hide.

"You okay, Matthew? You're looking a little off."

"I'm fine."

"Really? Because you look like you're gonna throw up."

"Yeah, I, uh, just gotta get back to the office. Catch you later."

I slammed my drink down and walked away knowing full well I was only making myself look even guiltier. And as I left the lounge, I was sure he could see inside my head and was positive he knew exactly what I was thinking.

That's it, you've officially gone nuts. David's a lawyer, not a freakin' psychic. He has no idea why you're acting so shifty.

Then why did he even bring up Becca? Did he suspect something? Was he fishing for info?

I speed-walked back to the office as though I was trying to run away from my own thoughts.

Paranoia doesn't suit you, Matthew. Get your shit together!

~

"What's up with you?" Sandra questioned the minute I walked into her sight.

"Nothing. Why?"

"You walked in here like your ass was on fire. Just thought I'd ask."

"Just have a lot of work to do." I strode passed her into my office, slamming the door closed behind me.

I had to get my head back in the game. I had to stop thinking about Becca and the photos and anything else that interfered with me running my multi-million-dollar corporation.

Looking at the clock, I saw I could at least get a few hours of correspondence done before my next meeting. All I had to do was put my head down and focus.

Pulling up my emails, I scanned the lines. The usual. Junk. Email from one of my equipment suppliers. Blah blah. Wait, what the fuck? For the second time that day, I was confronted with an email address made up of mysterious numbers and letters.

No. Not again.

I hoped it wasn't more photos and, with my blood pressure rising, I clicked on it. To my relief, there were no photos. But, to my sheer horror, I saw something so much worse. My eyes skimmed the words, then I read them again. Then again. Then one more time as my head began to spin.

This can't be saying what I think it is!

Suddenly, photographs of me and Becca kissing were the least of my worries.

You're a sick fuck. Think it's okay to sleep with a girl half your age? Well think again. I know everything about you. You've been grooming Becca since she was a child, haven't you? Just waiting for her to grow up so she could be your little fucktoy.

For a second, I was sure I was going to vomit. I could hear the blood pumping in my ears and my hands begin to sweat.

This can't be happening.

My first thought was to find whoever it was who sent the email and kick the living shit out of them. The second thought that crossed my mind was to call the cops.

But I hadn't called the cops in my life, not that I could remember anyway. What exactly was I supposed to do? Dial nine-one-one and ask them to investigate a nasty email? They'd probably just laugh in my face.

I know, I thought. *I'll head right on down to the nearest police station and explain it all calmly to an officer. I'll print off everything to show them and they'll understand how serious it is. And they can see who I am. Not some wacko on the end of the phone, but Matthew Banks from the commercials.*

I clicked the print button so hard I almost broke the mouse, and a second later, the photos and emails came spewing out. Clutching them tightly, the paper still hot and the ink still smelling fresh, I strode out passed Sandra again.

"Remember you have a meeting at four with Yamanoto," she said.

"Yep! I'll be back."

~

"Sir, I understand how frustrating this is for you, but there's not a whole lot we can do right now."

The officer behind the desk, a little squirt of a thing that barely looked old enough to graduate high school was flicking through my print outs.

I had handed them to him, hoping he would file them away as evidence, but he only thumbed through them disinterested.

"Someone's following me," I told him. "You've got to find out who it is."

He slid the pages back across the desk to me and leaned his elbows across the counter. "There's nothing we can really do," he said. "I mean, do you have any idea who it could be? If you did, I suppose we could talk to them."

"I have no idea who it is. That's why I'm here."

"Ah, yes. Obviously."

"So, what are you going to do?" He blinked at me in response. "I can hand over my computer to you if that makes things easier. Can't you get your techy wizard computer forensic folk to poke around and see where the email came from?"

"Hmm...that's not really how the forensics department works."

"What? Can't you find an IP address from the email or something? Anything at all?"

Still disinterested, he glanced at the clock as though I was holding him back from his break. Then, as though he couldn't get any more annoying, he yawned.

I wanted to reach across the counter and strangle the little shit. But I stopped myself. *Millionaire fitness tycoon strangles policeman* would not be a good headline for business.

"You can come back if things escalate," he said.

"Escalate? Escalates into what? The guy shoots me with a gun instead of a camera? Whoever this creep is, they're sending what could be perceived as threats to me. And they're accusing me of something I didn't do!"

"I know. I know. It's a bummer."

"A bummer? Are you serious? Look, I need this sorted today. I want you to find out who this person is. Got it? I'm a rich man. I don't know if I've made some sort of business enemy or someone thinks they can get some cash out of me or what. But I need you to act on this right now."

That seemed to get the message across to him and he twirled in his seat toward the computer.

"Name."

"Excuse me?"

"Your name."

"Matthew Banks."

I expected this would have roused some interest in him. That he would have seen my commercials and recognized me, but I would have no such luck.

"Contact details."

I rattled off my phone number and address and slid the print outs back over the desk.

"We'll see what we can do," he said, taking the photos and emails back. "But I can't promise anything. This is a big city, Mr. Banks. There's a lot of serious cases that need solved. We can't just send our lead detectives out to chase down a couple mean emails."

"They're not just mean emails," I explained, balling my hands into fists at my side. "They're evidence that I'm being stalked."

He acted as though he didn't hear me and reached over to a flimsy plastic shelf on the wall. Pulling out a leaflet, he handed it to me then slid lazily off his chair.

"Read this," he told me, dismissively adding, "And have a nice day."

Before I could say a word, he disappeared through the door into the back room. Looking down at the flier in my hand, I read the first line.

Are you a victim of internet bullying? Below the question was a stock image of a teenage girl sitting in bed crying.

"Asshole," I seethed, balling up the flier in my hand. Throwing it onto the desk, I stormed out, barging through the revolving doors.

If the police aren't gonna do shit, I'll find the bastard myself.

"Mr. Banks!" the man named Sean said in a thick Irish accent. "Seen your commercials on the TV."

He was sitting at his desk with a lit cigarette dangling from his thin, rubbery lips. A brown fedora was perched precariously on his head, a few straw-like strands of red hair poking out the edges. I got the impression it was more of a prop than a fashion statement.

There wasn't a single computer in the office. There was, however, an overflowing ashtray, a stack of brown envelopes, and something that looked as though it might be a pastrami sandwich that had been sitting for several hours.

"So, how can I help you?" he asked, knotting his sausage-like fingers together on the desk. "It's some private investigating you're wanting done, is it?"

He blew out smoke that stung my eyes and nose. I guess he didn't get the memo that smoking wasn't permitted in business establishments anymore, but it looked as though he missed a lot of memos.

"That's right," I said. "I was searching for a reputable private investigator and your name consistently came up."

But as I sat in his office, the smell of tobacco clinging to my clothes and my shoes sticking to the filthy carpet, I was starting to think all the online review were fake. This guy didn't look as though he knew how to find his way out of the nineteen-fifties let alone find my stalker.

"That's right," he said. "I use traditional methods of investigation. Have for decades now, and I find they get the best results."

"I like traditional methods," I murmured, feeling as though we may have more in common than I previously thought. "So, you can help me track down this piece of shit?"

"I can do more than find him," Sean assured me. "I'll find out his blood type, his mother's maiden name, and what size his feet are if you want."

I couldn't help but laugh. The old guy, as crusty as he was, was a breath of fresh, smoke-filled air. "I'll hold you to that," I said, reaching over to shake his hand. "Name your price. I'll pay you half now, half when the guy is caught."

He nodded solemnly as he reached into the top drawer of his desk and pulled out a notepad. On it, he began scrawling a number.

"This is my flat fee for every one of my clients," he explained. He pushed his notepad over to me and I read the number, which, to me, looked strangely modest.

"I'll double it if you can do it in half the time," I countered.

"I'll try my best."

"Pleasure doing business with you," I replied, shaking his hand for the second time.

"You won't be disappointed, Mr. Banks. I can guarantee that."

CHAPTER 19

BECCA

It was five to four and the boardroom was set up for the meeting. Everyone was there, ready and waiting, making awkward, polite small talk. Everyone except Matthew. He was nowhere to be seen.

"Please excuse me," I said to the room as I shuffled around the table and out the door.

Sandra was waiting at her desk, staring at the elevator doors as though she could summon Matthew out of them if she looked hard enough.

"Where is he?" I asked her.

"I was gonna ask you the same thing." Her tone was still bitter, her eyes icy.

"The meeting starts in four minutes," I worried aloud. "And Mr. Yamanoto and his associates have come all the way from Tokyo to meet with Matthew about expanding his brand in the East. If he's even ten seconds late, they'll freak."

"I'm well aware of that," Sandra snapped. "He'll be here. Sometimes he might cut it a bit close, but he always shows up."

I was growing more nervous by the second and couldn't

stand just waiting around. "I can't go back in the room without him," I said to Sandra. "I'm going into Matthew's office. He has some files saved on his computer I was waiting for him to print out anyway. May as well do them now."

Sandra raised one questioning eyebrow then another. "Oh, so he lets you just walk on into his office now, does he? And log on to his computer?"

"Yeah, he does," I replied, staring her down.

She stared back at me as though she was trying to set me on fire with her mind. Ignoring her, I entered his office and took a seat at his computer.

Shit, only three minutes to go. Where is he?

Logging into his computer, I tried to find the folder with the files, but to my horror, I saw he had seven tabs open already.

Jesus Christ. Has he never heard of canceling a page?

I ignored them and dragged the mouse across the desktop looking for the folder I needed. But instead of clicking on it, my finger slipped, and I accidentally tapped a random tab. His emails opened before I could stop it. I moved to click off it, but my eyes were drawn to the body of the email written in angry capital letters.

You've been grooming her since she was a child...

What the fuck? What lunatic sent this? And why didn't he tell me about this?

I was so in shock, so absorbed by what I was seeing, I didn't hear the door open.

"Becca?"

Frozen, I looked up with a hand clapped to my mouth.

"What are you doing?" Matthew asked looking down at his computer. "What's the matter?"

My eyes moved back to the email, then up to him. By the look on his face, he knew I had seen it.

"Who sent this?"

"I'm going to find out."

"This is beyond fucked up. You need to go to the cops."

"Believe me. I've been."

"And? Are they gonna find them?"

He let out a long sigh and massaged his temples with his fingertips as if he had a massive headache. "I'll find the asshole," he said. "You have my word I will."

"You better. They're obviously insane! What are they gonna do next?"

"Who the hell knows?"

"What if they get violent? They're already following us and now they're making crazy accusations and spewing this shit. I mean, what the hell? You and I both know you didn't groom me as a kid."

"Yeah, *we* both know that. But if they start spreading the rumor, do you think other people are gonna believe it?"

"Of course they won't! You're a good guy, Matthew. You're not some sleazy douche bag."

"But the public loves a rumor," he replied sadly. "And once one as serious as this comes out, people will always wonder if Matthew Banks groomed his best friend's daughter to be his little sex slave once she was of age."

"No one will think that!" I tried to convince him, but even I knew the public were fickle and loved gossip. And what better story was there than this?

"But it's not the public that scares me the most," he continued, moving around beside me. "It's your dad."

"You're his best friend. He loves you like a brother. He'll understand."

"I fucking doubt that. He'll kick my head in. He'll never forgive me for what I've done."

"What *we've* done," I corrected him. "It's not like I was some passive victim. I wanted it."

A look of understanding flashed between us. We both

wanted to be together. And knowing the trouble it could land us in seemed to bond us even closer, as though it was us two and our forbidden fucking against the world.

"What if this nutcase blows all this wide open?" he said, waving his hand angrily at the screen. "What if he tells your father?"

"My dad will understand. He loves me and wants me to be happy. I mean, sure, he'll be shocked, but he'll get over it. I'm sure he will."

"I think you're delusional," he laughed mockingly. "Your dad will have an aneurysm if he finds out and you know it!"

We fell silent for a second, each of us contemplating what to do next. I knew what was on Matthew's mind. He was thinking *Let's hush everything up and pretend it never happened. Let's make sure Bob never finds out a thing.* But I was thinking the complete opposite.

"I think we should tell him," I announced, projecting all my strength into the statement.

Matthew looked at me warily for a second as though he thought I'd grown a second head.

"Tell him," I repeated. "If he finds out from whoever this person is, it'll be catastrophic, but if it comes from us..." I let the sentence die as I shrugged.

"It'll still be catastrophic."

"But not so much of a shock," I pointed out. "And, he's going to find out eventually, right? How long can we hide this?"

Forever, said his eyes, but his mouth said, "I suppose he'll find out eventually."

"So we'll tell him?"

He clutched at his hair and looked out the window across the city. I noticed he was staring in the direction of Dad's gym.

"Matthew. I'm not sure exactly what's happening between

us, but I know *something* is happening. And it's intense and it's raw and it's the best thing I've ever experienced. We're amazing together. And I think my dad deserves to know that."

His eyes glossed over as he disappeared inside his own head. He remained in a daydream for a second, and just when I thought he'd never come out of it, he snapped and looked at me. He took my hand and brushed my hair behind my ear, pulling me closer to him.

"We are amazing together, aren't we?" he said. "You're right. He has to know, but I can tell you, this isn't going to go well. I wouldn't be surprised if he knocked me flat on my ass. He's a boxer, remember?"

"He won't touch you. Let me do all the talking."

"Are you sure?"

"Positive."

"Okay," he said and took in a deep breath. "What's the worst that can happen?"

"Exactly. What's the worst that can happen?"

"Hey!" A loud voice and a bang from the door announced Sandra as she barged in. "I don't know what the hell is so urgent in here, but Yamanoto is on the cusp of shitting kittens if you don't hurry up."

"I'm coming," Matthew said, pulling away from me. "Just give me a second."

Sandra grumbled in response, but she ignored him completely as she glared at me. I darted my eyes from the email on the screen to her angry face.

Was Sandra actually crazy enough to send it?

CHAPTER 20

MATTHEW

How did I let her talk me into this? This is the worst idea I've ever had in my whole fucking life!

What's the worst that can happen? Well, Bob could actually kill me. Didn't he say he used to keep a gun in the house? If there was ever a time to grab it, it would be now.

"Are you okay?" Bob asked across the table. He was chewing on a piece of steak, giving his jaw a good workout on the slab of meat that was still bleeding.

"Yeah, man I'm good."

"You looked miles away there," he said. "And you haven't touched your steak."

I looked down at my plate where my favorite, a sirloin steak slathered in peppercorn sauce, sat untouched. Usually I would have devoured it in minutes, but tonight my stomach was churning.

"Are you not feeling well?"

"I'm fine," I said and stabbed my fork into the steak.

Beside me, Becca was nibbling on a broccoli stem looking as sweet as apple pie. Could she have looked anymore innocent if she tried? With no makeup, her hair tied in a high bun and her office clothes replaced with skinny jeans and a hooded sweatshirt, she looked like a teenager. As I watched her eat, I noticed no trace of the powerful office boss I saw at work.

Her eyes met mine, and she offered a cute little smile. Below the table, her hand made its way to my thigh and I shot her a panicked look.

Is she nuts? What if her dad sees?

"So this is a real nice idea of Becca to invite you over for dinner," Bob said as he sipped his beer. "I don't think I see you enough these days. You work too much, you know that?"

"I know. I should take a day off eventually."

"You're damn right you should. You should actually take some time to enjoy all that money you've been making. Christmas is coming up in a couple weeks. That would be the perfect excuse for a vacation."

I shoved a mouthful of steak into my mouth and savored the taste. I mumbled through the bite, "Fuck me, Bob. This is your best one yet. You've been working on the recipe like your life depends on it. What's your secret ingredient?"

He laughed, a great chuckle from somewhere deep in his gut and slapped his stomach. "I'm taking my secret ingredient to the grave," he said. "Nobody, and I mean nobody, is gonna find out what it is."

"It's ketchup," Becca revealed, giggling.

Bob instantly stopped laughing and glared at her as though she'd just insulted his great ancestors. "Becca!"

"What? It's true. You put ketchup in everything."

"If you must know, it's ketchup and soy sauce," Bob clarified. "There. You have it now. Bob's big meat marinade secret is out."

I knew he was only joking, but he looked genuinely hurt at the revelation.

Shit, if he's this worked up about a steak recipe, how's he gonna react to finding out about Becca and me?

With a huge fake smile plastered on my face, I tried to direct the topic of conversation toward something happy to put him in a good mood.

"So Becca's doing great in the office," I announced. "She's a natural in a corporate environment. Takes to it like a duck to water."

Bob smiled and set his fork down as he reached for the hot sauce. "She gets that from her mom. She was a real brainy girl. Not like me at all. I can barely spell let alone do all that fancy corporate stuff. That shit would fry my brain."

He threw a worryingly large amount of hot sauce onto his place and scooped it up with a French fry.

"But I'm real happy," he said as he chewed. "You wouldn't even believe how glad I am to have her working for you. Not only is her first job outta college a good one, but it's with my best buddy. I mean, how much better can it get?"

Becca began laughing nervously, and I couldn't help but join in, the two of us giggling like idiots.

"Besides," Bob continued, unconcerned with our strange laughter. "I'm just so happy Becca's with someone I can trust. Someone who I know will treat her with respect. I mean, guys are freakin' creeps, right? I know how women get treated in the workplace. Like they're just there for eye candy. At least it's not like that with you, eh Matthew?"

"No, of course not!" I spat out with a bit too much enthusiasm. "It's not like that at all." I shot Becca a worried glance and noticed she was holding her breath. "Sorry, I just have to go to the bathroom," I blurted, screeching my chair back from the table.

"Get us another beer on the way back?" Bob asked.

"Sure."

I edged around him feeling as though my insides were

melting, and the very second I entered the hallway, I let out a huge, exasperated sigh. Hurrying to the bathroom, I locked the door behind me and stared into the mirror.

"Fuck," was all I could say.

Running the taps, I splashed my face with cold water and tried to calm down.

You can't tell him.

Unless Becca's telling him right now.

Oh, God what if I get back in the kitchen and she's told him everything?

Reaching for the towel, I dried my face. A gentle, timid knock sounded from the door and I lowered the towel from my face.

"Hello?"

"It's me," Becca said.

I opened the door a crack and she barged right in, slamming the door behind her.

"What are you doing?" I whispered angrily. "What if your dad catches us in here together?"

"Chill! He went into the garage to get the ice cream. We'll be safe for the next two minutes."

I didn't feel safe at all.

"We can't tell him," she said. "Not now. Not after what he just said."

"Agreed. It's literally the worst possible time. But how long can we keep this a secret?"

She smiled and wrapped one arm around my neck, lowering the other hand to my crotch. I instantly hardened in her grasp.

"You are out of your fucking mind," I said, shoving her hand away. "Are you trying to get us in trouble?"

"Hey guys! Where did you go? I got ice cream!" Bob yelled from the kitchen.

"Coming!" Becca called. She kissed me hard, rubbing her

hand up my erect cock, then slipped out the door and to the kitchen.

"Mint chocolate chip. Yum!" I heard her say.

That girl is going to give me a heart attack, I thought as I leaned against the door. *She's nothing but trouble.*

CHAPTER 21

BECCA

I woke up to my phone's alarm mingling with the sound of freezing rain lashing the windows. It was one of those perfect Sunday mornings where the weather roared like a hurricane outside and the trees sounded as though they were ready to snap in the wind. But I could stay in bed for as long as I wanted.

Turning off the alarm, I luxuriated beneath my warm comforter and let out a satisfied sigh. I'd been working like a dog all week, and there was nothing I wanted more than to just chill and take it easy.

My only plans for the day was a girly brunch booked in a cute little French place in town with Janey, but that wasn't for at least another three hours. Until then, I could lie on my ass and dream away the morning. Hell, I might even have to run a hot bath and light a few candles. Was there a better way to spend a Sunday morning?

I closed my eyes again, but just as I started to drift off to sleep, my phone buzzed with a message from Janey.

Still on for brunch today?

I texted back. *Wouldn't miss it for the world.*

As I moved to lock my phone screen, I noticed the date. The day usually sprung upon me, leaving me with a feeling of dread, and it had done so since I was at least twelve years old. Unlike most girls, my period ran like freakin' clockwork. You could almost set your watch to it. And it always started on the morning of the twenty eighth day of my cycle with killer stomach cramps and an insatiable appetite for anything with chocolate in it.

But I wasn't feeling like that this morning, and there wasn't a single hint of a cramp.

Weird... Could I have really struck it lucky and stopped getting cramps?

I doubted it. They were a curse and I didn't think they'd suddenly take off this month when they'd plagued me for most of my life.

Checking the date again, I confirmed it was definitely the twenty eighth day. So where the hell was my period? I couldn't believe that for the first time ever, I was actually wishing my period would hurry up. It just felt so wrong to not feel my usual symptoms that told me everything was working perfectly down there.

Trying to not worry about it, I shoved my thoughts to the back of my mind and got up to enter the bathroom where I ran the bath.

You need to chill. All this hard work and long hours has probably done a number on your body. Stress can wreak havoc with your cycle. Yeah, that's it. It's just stress. Nothing else. Just chill.

As I sank into the hot water and stared up at the ceiling, watching wisps of steam drift up over the tiles, I took a deep breath and tried to relax.

"Just stress," I said out loud, sinking into the tub and putting it out of my mind. I'd probably start tomorrow.

~

"Hiyeee!"

Janey was waiting at the table sipping on a White Russian when I blustered in through the door with my inside out umbrella and my scarf wrapped around my face.

"You're late!" she moaned as she stood up to hug me.

"Took me about ten years to find a parking space and the weather's a nightmare." I sat down and smoothed the rain from my hair. "It's good to see you started early," I said, pointing at her drink. "Where's mine?"

"On its way," she said, and right on cue, the waiter appeared with a Mimosa on a silver tray.

"Oh, Janey, you read my mind." I took it from the tray and didn't let it hit the table. I took a long sip and closed my eyes to savor the taste. "I've needed this. This week's been a real bitch."

"Really? Matthew not the dream boss you thought he was?"

"Actually, he's great. It's just the work load's a bit crazy. That's all."

"Already? You've only been there like a month? How much responsibility can he have given you?"

"A lot," I replied with a laugh. "He seems to think I'm capable of doing more than your average new girl."

"Well, that's a good thing, right? It means you're obviously capable of doing it all. Maybe you'll even get a promotion soon."

"Hopefully," I thought out loud. "But right now, we're just focusing on this meeting we have coming up. You know Matthew's got his heart set on expanding the company?"

Janey nodded as she sucked on her straw. "What did you say his plan was? Open a new gym a month for the next two years?"

"Yeah, that's the plan. The only problem is that he needs capital to expand. Anyway, to cut a long story short, we've got a meeting next week with potential investors, two billionaires from New York who are like royalty in the fitness world. If he can win them over, he'll be sorted for life."

"And so will you," Janey added with a wink. "The money will trickle down hopefully. Anyway, I'm sure you'll do great. Matthew's already a big name. It's not as if he's some nobody going on *Shark Tank* to claw some crumbs off the table."

"That's what I thought. I think he'll ace the meeting, but you know what he's like. He's a perfectionist. So he's freaking out right now. Trying to make sure every tiny detail is accounted for. It's driving me nuts. You'd think we were going to war, not having a business meeting."

She was listening, but I could tell she was distracted. Her eyes were sadly looking into her glass and her shoulders were slumped forward as though she was ready to fall asleep on the table.

"You okay?" I asked her, leaning over to pat her arm.

"I'm fine. Why?"

"You look tired."

"Tired of Harry's bullshit."

Shocked, I breathed, "Whoa, where did that come from? I thought everything was great with you two."

She shot me an angry look that dissolved into sadness. "We were," she replied. "But...shit, I still love him more than anything. It's just that, I dunno, as we've gotten older and moved in together it's not quite what I hoped it would be. I spend most of my time being more like his mother than a girlfriend, and he spends most of his time out drinking with his buddies. It's like he's..."

"Taking you for granted?" I suggested.

She nodded and took a long sip of her drink. "That's exactly it."

"Get rid of him," I told her.

There was nothing else to say. If my best girl was

unhappy because of that douche bag, then I wanted him out of her life.

"I can't just leave him!" she squealed.

"Sure, you can."

"No, I can't! We've been together for years!"

"So? Just because you hooked up in high school doesn't mean you're destined to be together forever."

Her face crumpled as she looked into her glass. It was empty now, and she sighed heavily. "I always thought it would be forever."

A waiter arrived and, sensing the atmosphere at the table, hung back for a second. "Shall I give you two a few minutes?"

"No, it's okay," Janey said. "I'll have the French toast with the blueberries."

"Sounds great. I'll have the same."

He gave us both a polite smile and a curt nod then disappeared into the kitchen. As I watched him leave, I was acutely aware of Janey staring into the side of my face. As I turned to meet her gaze, she glanced away.

"What?"

"Nothing."

"You were looking at me weird."

"I was just thinking you look really pretty today," she said.

"Aw, really?"

"Sure. You're all glowy," she replied, waving her hands over her cheeks. "Like you've been on vacation. Either that or..."

"What?"

"You've been getting it good from someone."

I blushed and looked down at the table.

"There is someone, isn't there?" she squeaked, forgetting her sadness in her excitement.

"No..."

"Cut the crap, Becca. I know there is. Over the last few

weeks your head's been up your ass. Like you've got your mind on that good dick."

"Janey!"

"Who is he?"

"No one!"

"Shut up. Just tell me who it is."

"No!"

"So there is someone!"

"I didn't say that."

"Shit, is it someone from the office?" she asked, excitedly. "Some super hot gym hunk?"

I didn't reply, but the look in my eyes answered for me.

"It is!" she laughed, her eyes widening. "I can't believe you've been seeing someone and haven't told me."

"I haven't really been *seeing* him," I said, my mind drifting to Matthew. Images of his naked body came to mind along with the feel of his arms around me and the sensation of his lips on my neck, my breasts. "It's just a casual thing," I told her. "Nothing to write home about."

"By the look on your face you've got a lot to write home about. Why didn't you tell me about him?"

"Like I said. It was just a casual thing."

"Just an office fling?"

"Yeah, something like that." That wasn't what I wanted it to be, but that's what I was going with.

"Do you think something more will happen between you?" she asked. She'd perked up and had forgotten all about Harry for the moment.

"I don't think so," I said. "It's complicated."

"Oh no! Don't tell me he's with someone else. Shit, he's not married, is he?"

"No! No, he's definitely single."

"Aw, Becca. I'm so happy for you. I can really see you like him a lot. Even if you are just trying to play it cool."

"Shit, is my poker face really that bad?"

"It's freakin' terrible."

We both laughed, and a moment later the waiter returned with our food. "Bon Appetit," he said as he placed down my plate.

I was hit by the smell of warm cream, melted butter, and horribly unhealthy fried goodness. "I really shouldn't be eating this," I said. "I've been treating myself a bit too much recently."

"You only live once. Go nuts."

As I stared at the plate, I felt overwhelmed with hunger and began stabbing violently into my French toast and devouring it like it was the last meal on Earth.

"Wow, what's got into you?" Janey laughed as she watched me shoveling my food into my mouth. "It looks like you haven't eaten for a week."

Realizing my plate was already half empty, I slowed down and began nibbling on the blueberries.

"It's awesome to see you with such an appetite," Janey said, licking whipped cream off her fork. "Remember when you were in college and you were all hung up about your weight? And you'd have a meltdown if you put on a single pound."

"I still feel like that sometimes."

"Yeah, well, you shouldn't because you look incredible. Honestly, your skin is like an angel's today. What foundation are you wearing?"

"Just the usual."

"Shut up. Is it a new serum, then?"

"Nope. Seriously, I've done nothing to my skin."

"If I didn't know you better, I'd assume you'd got some fancy thing done to your face. Like that crazy one they do with all the needles, or when they scrape your face with a scalpel."

"You're nuts," I laughed. "I haven't done a thing to my skin."

"Then you must be pregnant," she joked. "I remember when my sister had her first baby her skin glowed like she was a supermodel or something."

"Well, I can happily rule that out. There's no way I could be pregna...."

But as the words came out of my mouth, it felt like a lead weight had been dropped into my stomach.

"Hey, you okay?" Janey asked, staring at me.

For a second, I felt as though I couldn't speak, and I just stared into the distance with my jaw dropped open.

"Becca. You're scaring me."

"I'm...okay," I managed to say.

"Really? Because you look like you've just seen a ghost."

"No, this can't be happening. I can't be pregnant."

Reaching across the table, she grabbed my arms and pulled me toward her, her eyes wide. "Did you use protection?" The look in my eyes said it all. "Shit, Becca! Are you kidding me? You're not on the pill?" I shook my head. "And he didn't use a condom?"

"No but, um…"

"But what?"

"Shit. What have I done? What do I do?"

"You take a test is what you do. Right now."

"Right now?"

"Yes. Right now."

We sat on the edge of my bath staring at the unopened pregnancy test in my hand.

"Just hurry up and do it," Janey urged.

"I'm getting to it. I'm just thinking."

"There's nothing to think about. Just whip it out and pee."

"There's a *lot* to think about," I replied. "What if it's positive?"

"If it is, the sooner you find out the better."

I sighed and shook my head. "You're right."

I tore the cellophane off the box and let the test slide out into my hand.

"Are you going to give me some privacy?" I asked. "Or do you fancy being my audience?"

"Sorry," she smiled apologetically and stood up. "I'll go make some tea."

She slipped out of the room, leaving me alone. Except I didn't feel alone because the test felt so huge and important it almost had its own presence.

"Okay, just do it," I told myself, pulling down my pants. "You have to know."

After peeing on the stick, I sat for a moment, staring as though the harder I squinted, the faster the test would work.

"You okay in there?" Janey asked with a knock on the door.

"I feel like I'm having a heart attack."

"Have you done it yet?"

I reached over and unlocked the door. "Yeah. Just have the dreaded two minutes to wait."

With the test clenched in my hand, I walked to the living room and sat on the couch. The same couch Matthew had taken my virginity on. It seemed like a fitting place to discover the news. I looked at my Christmas tree and wondered if I was about to get one hell of a Christmas surprise.

"So are you going to tell me who it is?" Janey asked, setting cups of tea down on the coffee table.

I said nothing, my eyes glued to the test. How long had passed? A minute? A year? It felt like a lifetime.

"Take that as a no then," she said and sat beside me. "Do you think the father will want to know? Do you think he'll step up and take responsibility?"

Father. The word sounded so adult and formal. What would Matthew think of being called a father? Did he even want to be one? I supposed he didn't. After all, if he wanted to have children, wouldn't he have had them with Olivia? At his age he could have started a family over twenty years ago.

I looked back down at the test and saw a hint of pink appear in a faint line.

Oh, God it's happening. Any second now I'm going to know if I'm going to be a mother.

And in that second, between dreading and knowing, I suddenly found a voice at the back of my brain asking, *Would it be so bad if it was positive? Haven't you always wanted to be a mother?*

Slowly, the two of us leaned closer to the test as the pink grew more vivid. We watched as the first line developed before it was joined a second later by another, just as pink and vivid as the first.

I checked the box, looked back at the test, checked the box again, then sighed. "I'm pregnant."

Janey hugged me, the two of us latching onto each other for dear life.

"I don't know whether to laugh or cry!" I whispered, hugging her tight. "What the hell do I do now?"

CHAPTER 22

MATTHEW

"Morning, Sandra."

"Hello, Matthew. There's someone in your office to see you."

"Already? It's barely eight."

"I know, but he seemed pretty persistent. Irish fella. Told him to wait in your office."

Sean, I thought as I strode toward my door. *He's got news for me already? And it must be big if he's here this early.*

Entering my office, I found him sitting in the armchair in the corner that had purely been decorative until now. In one hand he was holding a cup of coffee while in the other he gripped a brown envelope. "Hello, Sean. Good to see you."

"How are you?" he asked, shaking my hand with his calloused fingers after depositing the envelope on the table.

"Good, but by the look on your face my mood's about to drop."

"Perhaps," he said, handing me the envelope. "It's not good news I'm coming to tell ya."

I took the envelope and tore it open. Freshly printed

paper slipped out into my hand. "What is this?" I asked, looking at a jumble of computer code.

"I traced the IP address from your nasty emails," he said. "And not only that, but those sneaky photographs of you that you received held a surprising amount of data."

"Really? Please tell me you found out who's behind this." I flipped through the papers and couldn't make heads nor tails of all the letters and numbers.

"Check the last page," he said. "You'll see an address corresponding to the IP."

I did as he suggested and flicked through. My eyes quickly scanned the page as my heartbeat quickened. "Seven-three-five Marlborough Boulevard," I read out loud. "That's where the emails came from?"

Sean nodded and ran a hand over his head and leveled a grim look at me. "I'm assuming you know who resides there?" he asked as recognition dawned on my face.

"Olivia." I was stunned for a second, too shocked to speak. "You're sure this information is correct?"

He nodded. "Yes sir. I checked and rechecked to be sure. It's correct." He slipped his hat on top of his head and aimed for the door. "I'm sorry. I'm sure you weren't expecting someone so close to home to be behind this. But if I'm being honest, I've been in this game long enough to know ex-wives and husbands can be capable of just about anything. This is rather tame in comparison to some of the stuff I've seen."

"Tame?"

Was being accused of basically being a pedophile tame? Was being followed and photographed no big deal?

"Yeah, tame," he repeated. "Anyhow, I best be on my way."

"I suppose I should thank you," I said, shaking his hand although I had no idea what I had to be grateful for.

As he left, I sunk into my seat and tried to process it all. But I couldn't believe what I was seeing. Out of all the people

I thought could be behind it, I never once suspected her. I mean, sure, she was a bitch and a terrible wife. But was she really capable of such an awful accusation?

I guessed she was.

But why? What the fuck did she think she was going to get from this?

Then it dawned on me. The divorce settlement. She'd made it pretty clear she didn't think she was getting enough, so what did she decide to do? Blackmail me to get more money.

A gentle knock sounded on the door, followed by a soft voice I instantly recognized it as Becca's.

"Come in."

She entered with a slight smile. With her coat and scarf on, she was still wrapped up for the outdoors, but I couldn't help but notice underneath all the wool her face was glowing.

"Just wanted to pick up those notes you made for our preparation for the investor meeting."

"Sure."

I noticed her eyes land on Sean's findings on the desk and before she could see any more, I dumped a large folder on top. As soon as I handed her my notes, she turned and walked away. There was no denying her urgency to leave my office. Over the last week, she had been distant, almost disinterested in me unless it was to discuss work.

But of course she was disinterested. She was a beautiful, driven and phenomenal twenty-three-year-old. What was I to her apart from some crusty old dude, her boss, her dad's best buddy? She'd probably met someone closer to her own age, someone with as much energy as she had and who at least knew how to work Instagram unaided.

"Catch you later," she said, walking out the door without turning back.

I heard the authoritative stride of her high heels as they smacked off the hallway floor.

She's over you, I thought as I closed the door behind her. *She's moved on.*

I just wished I could say the same about Olivia.

CHAPTER 23

BECCA

The day passed in a haze of meetings, paperwork, and cups of decaf coffee, which was completely useless. But no matter how busy I was, I couldn't get Matthew out of my head. Or rather, I couldn't get what I had to tell him out my head. As I tried to focus on my work, my brain wouldn't shut up.

You have to tell him he's going to be a father.

But as much as I knew I had to tell him, there was a devil sitting on my other shoulder telling me not to.

He hasn't got time for kids. Not to mention he's probably not interested in you anymore. He's barely looked at you in days or said a word unless it's about work.

As the clock reached six, I grabbed my things and headed for the elevator.

"Good night," a happy though exhausted voice came from behind me. Looking around, I saw Matthew in his doorway with a briefcase in his hand. "I'm just heading home in a minute. I can give you a ride if you want."

For a second, I almost said yes, then I stopped myself.

Keep your distance for now. Think before you get close to him again.

"No thank you. I have my car," I said, pressing the button for the elevator.

"Oh, okay."

"See you tomorrow."

If I wasn't mistaken, there was a deeply disappointed look in his eyes, but as soon as I noticed it, it was gone.

Stepping in the elevator, I felt his gaze on me as the doors slid shut. Turning to see my reflection in the mirror, I was surprised but pleased to see what Janey had said was true.

Holy shit, my skin does look amazing.

Downstairs, I hurried to the parking lot and found my car. In the distance, I could make out Matthew's Porsche in the corner. *Better get going before he gets down here,* I thought as I twisted the key in the ignition.

Driving home, I lost myself in thought as I drifted along the dark road filled nose to tail with impatient rush hour drivers.

"Come on, come on."

My head was in a spin. No matter how much I tried to think sensibly, there was always some chaotic part of my brain telling me to do the opposite.

You have to tell him.

No, never tell him.

Are you even going to keep the baby? Of course you are. You've always wanted to be a mother. But now's not the right time, is it? Is there ever really a right time?

I arrived home exhausted and trudged up to my apartment. Somehow, every movement felt different, every physical sensation putting me on edge. It was as though I was hyper aware of my body and what it contained. Deep inside me, I was carrying something so precious I had to guard it at all costs.

Once inside, I locked the door and did what I always did when my mind was a mess. Ran a bath. I spun the taps and watched the tub fill up as I poured in a generous amount of rose oil.

Just relax, I thought as I peeled off my clothes. *There's no rush to do anything right now. There's no harm in taking your time and thinking things through.*

But as I lay in the water and waited for the calming, soothing sensation of the heat to wash over me, I noticed it didn't come.

What are you doing just lying here? Don't you know you have to tell Matthew about the baby? The longer you wait the worse it's going to get!

"Fuck!"

Unable to relax, I dragged myself out the tub and wrapped a towel around me. Out in the hall, I grabbed my cellphone off the table and dialed Matthew's number. I was a little lightheaded as he answered and held my breath as I thought about what to say.

"Are you busy? I need to see you tonight, can't wait," I said in one frantic breath.

"Umm," he replied. "Sure...you wanna come over?"

"Yes. Yes, I want to come over."

"I'll call you a car," he offered.

For some reason I just knew he was smiling. I could hear it in the tone of his voice. Could almost feel it in my bones.

"See you soon," I said, and before I could change my mind, I hung up.

"Fuuuuuck!"

I knew Matthew was rich, but I had no idea he was like superstar rich. I'd read about his neighborhood before from celebrity blogs and social media, but I had never been up this way until now.

As the car approached the gates to Matthew's home, I gawped at the size of his house. It looked more like a palace than someone's home. And to think he lived here on his own? It must get lonely.

I fished in my purse for some cash for the driver, but before I could hand it over, Matthew's figure appeared at the side of the car.

"Here, keep the change," he said, handing a hundred dollar bill to the driver.

I climbed out of the car and gingerly approached him. Out of his suit, he was dressed casually in gray sweatpants and a black sweatshirt. Somehow, he was even hotter than usual. If that was even possible.

"Hey."

"Hey."

Now in front of him, I had no idea what to say.

Do I blurt it all out now? Or do I wait until we've gotten comfortable inside.

As I took a deep breath, I could feel my throat close up.

"Come inside," he said. "I'll give you the grand tour."

"Whoa! You have your own Olympic standard swimming pool in your basement?"

"I have two. One on this side of the house and one on the other."

"That's insane! Why two?"

"Olivia wanted one as well."

I assumed he was joking for a second, then I realized he wasn't. "Wow."

"Come on. I'll show you to my favorite room."

As he led me back up the stairs, I struggled to fathom a room better than the one we'd just left. As we climbed up the winding marble staircase, I struggled to comprehend how someone could live in all this space alone.

"It's just so freakin' huge," I gasped. "Do you not get lonely in here?"

"Occasionally," he replied, but his eyes said *all the time.* "Come on. I'll take you up."

We reached the top of the stairs and emerged in the center of a large, marble hallway.

"In here," Matthew said, opening a set of double doors.

I wondered what grandeur they could hide, but as I poked my head inside the room, I was confronted with something that wasn't grand at all, but cozy and almost normal.

"The lounge," he announced. "You look disappointed."

"Not disappointed, just... surprised. It's nothing like the other rooms in the house."

"That's the idea. I wanted this place to be like your average family room. Just a nice cozy place to hang out. Except there's one thing in here no average house has."

Flicking on the lights, he walked to the center of the room to what looked like a velvet pit.

"Is that a couch?"

"It's a sunken sofa," he said. "The largest sofa on the market. Come on, take your shoes off and jump in."

He dived into the center of the pillows like a big kid, and I laughed and jumped in after him. After getting comfortable, I looked at his happy face and said, "This is awesome."

"Nothing better than lying in this thing with a good movie on and a tub of ice cream."

"You? Ice cream?"

"Low fat."

"Obviously."

For a second, I almost forgot what I had come here to tell

him. Almost. I tried to get comfortable as he turned on the TV, but I couldn't relax.

Why did he bring me in here? What is he expecting?

"You okay?" he asked, settling on what looked like an old horror movie.

"Yeah. It's just that I have to tell you something."

Here it comes. Just blurt it out. You have to tell him.

Opening my mouth slightly, I prepared myself for telling him those two magic words that were going to change everything.

I'm pregnant.

Just spit it out!

But as I was about to speak, I felt his hand move toward my leg. It wasn't a sleazy gesture, but rather a soft, kind touch because he seemed genuinely happy I was there.

"I know I'm going to sound soft," he said. "But I've missed hanging out with you. I mean, I know we've been in the office together, but it's just not the same."

"No. It's not."

"That night out we had. It was great to talk and eat and have fun. I've wanted to do it again for a few weeks, but I guessed you'd moved on."

"Moved on? What? You think I got bored of you or something?"

"Got bored. Found someone else. Decided you didn't want to hang around with some old guy like me anymore."

"You're insane!" I gasped, leaning closer to him. "Matthew, there is nobody else. How could there be? You're my first. I can't just move on from that so easily." I leaned against him, holding my hands against his chest.

"You're young, you're beautiful, and you're fiercely intelligent," he said. "I wouldn't blame you."

"And you're Matthew Banks. The man I've wanted since I knew how to want a man."

He smiled and rested his hands on mine, holding them closer to him. His lips met mine tenderly. A soft groan escaped him as I brushed my tongue against his.

Okay, you can't let this go any further without telling him. He has to know about the baby.

But my body was overriding my brain, and the more I tried to pull away, the harder I kissed him.

Soon, we sank into the velvet abyss, our bodies melting into one another. I pulled him down on top of me, felt the weight and strength of his body on top of mine. Beneath him, I felt protected by him, almost owned by him. I wanted to give him everything.

Tearing at his clothes, I pulled his shirt over his head and kissed the muscles of his chest, relishing the chance to taste him, to feel the heat of his skin again.

His hands glided down me slowly but firmly, his fingers finding their way into the waistband of my jeans. With his lips caressing my neck, he pulled them down over my hips before tossing them to the side. I could feel how hard his cock was as it pressed into my thigh.

My panties were soaked through as he pulled them off, and he looked between my legs with a slight smirk on his lips. He knew how wet I was and what power he had over me.

Releasing his cock from his boxer shorts, he stroked it gently for a moment, his eyes scanning my body. Then he lowered himself and held me close in his strong arms. I had never felt so surrounded in warmth and safety. And as his lips met mine again and his cock pushed its way inside me, a thought entered my brain that eclipsed all others.

I love him.

I tried to push it out of my head, but as he thrust into me, his muscular arms holding me in place, I looked up at him and knew I could never force my feelings away. I was in love with him, and I couldn't deny it.

With a low moan, he fucked me gently, his eyes boring into mine as I surrendered my body to pleasure. Pure bliss washed over me in waves with every thrust, and it wasn't long before I could feel my first orgasm start to burn low in my belly.

"Cum for me," he whispered in my ear, sliding his hand down to my clit. He rubbed it gently, his tongue flicking over the lobe of my ear. "Cum for me, Becca."

I reached an instant, hard, brain melting orgasm that left my body shuddering beneath him until I was weak.

"That's my girl," he said, his breath hot on my neck. "You're so fucking hot when you cum like that. Shit Becca, I'm gonna cum."

He clenched his eyes shut and grit his teeth hard until his jaw looked ready to snap. Then he pulled himself taut from head to toe, a roar escaping his mouth as he came.

"Oh, God!" he breathed with a shudder, laying on top of me.

I spread my legs wider and wrapped them around his waist, pulling him closer to me.

I love you, I wanted to say. *I love you and I'm going to have your baby.*

But I couldn't get the words out. So I just closed my eyes and held him tight, wishing he would never get off me. Wishing he could hold me forever.

Slowly, he rose off me, but his eyes never left my face. He stared at me like I was made of gold. As if I was the most precious thing on Earth. His lips twitched as he moved to speak, his eyes filled with admiration.

"Becca, I..." He paused for a second, as though he wasn't sure if he should finish the sentence. Lifting my hand to his face, I caressed his jaw, urging him to continue.

"What Matthew?"

He stared deep into my eyes with an intensity that took my breath away. "I think I love you," he revealed, tracing a line with his finger down between my breasts. "I do. I really love you."

His eyes flicked back up to mine expectantly.

"I love you too," I whispered back. "I always have."

I opened my eyes and saw pure darkness. For a second, I thought I was still in bed in my apartment, but as my eyes adjusted to the shadows, I remembered where I was.

From the lounge we had made our way upstairs before sinking into the luxurious comfort of his king size bed. Feeling a raging thirst, I sat up and could vaguely see the outlines of the furniture.

There was an antique wardrobe at the back of the room, something that looked better suited to housing muskets and swords rather than sweaters.

I slipped out of bed naked. My feet sunk into the plush carpet, and for a second, I wiggled my toes and relished the softness. Still naked, I stepped out of the room and looked down the hallway, trying to remember what direction the kitchen was.

Moving through the house, I crept forward slowly and carefully until I found the staircase leading down to the first floor. My toes felt the slight coolness of the marble steps as I started to descend, and as I drifted down, I felt like I was in a movie, or a rather erotic fairy tale. Just a naked nymph fluttering down a marble spiral staircase.

At last, I found the kitchen, and with it, the ice maker and water dispenser on the side of the fridge. Filling up a glass, I took a big gulp and felt the refreshing iciness as it slipped down my throat.

I leaned against the counter, looking out toward the back garden. It was pure black out there, and for a fleeting second, I had the strangest sensation that someone was out there looking in.

Don't be silly, I told myself. *Nobody's out there. They couldn't get through the security gate.*

But still, I couldn't help but remember the stalker who took our picture. Were they out there watching now?

Suddenly, my nakedness didn't feel so glamorous anymore, and instead I felt vulnerable. Moving back into the lounge, I grabbed a blanket from the couch pit and wrapped it around my body.

Deciding I needed more water, I returned to the kitchen to fill up the glass, this time under the protection of the blanket should anyone be looking through the window.

There's nobody out there, I tried to reason. *You're just being paranoid.*

So why are the hairs on the back of my neck sticking up?

Why do I feel as though something is dreadfully wrong?

Hoping my anxiety stemmed from being tired, I wrapped the blanket around me tighter, clutched my glass and hurried for the stairs. Yet as soon as my foot hit the bottom step, I was aware of a scuffling noise behind me.

Footsteps.

I tried to turn to look, but before I could even move an inch, a heavy hand landed across my mouth.

"Don't make a fucking noise," a voice grunted in my ear. "You're coming with me."

Like hell I am! I thought. I may have been more afraid than I'd ever been in my life, but I wasn't going to let whoever this was capture me. I wriggled as hard as I could, the glass dropping from my hand and smashing on the floor.

But the arms around me wouldn't budge, and no matter how much I tried to fight, it was like I was being held in an iron grip.

Gradually, I could feel myself being dragged across the floor, my bare feet being pulled through the broken glass.

"Let me go!" I tried to scream through their hand.

"Shut the fuck up!" the person hissed, and a second later, a searing pain penetrated my left temple as everything turned black and I lost control of my limbs.

The last thing I felt before I lost consciousness completely was the sensation of the cold wind drifting up under my blanket and my face being peppered by snowflakes.

CHAPTER 24

MATTHEW

I woke up and flung my arm across the bed in search of Becca's body. When it fell flat against the cold bed sheets, I sat up and looked toward the en suite bathroom expecting to see her in there. But the door was open with no sign of her in the shower.

"Becca?"

Maybe she went downstairs for some breakfast.

Looking at the clock, I saw it was just passed six in the morning. She couldn't have been in a hurry to get up, could she?

Pulling on my bath robe, I ventured down to the kitchen, which I also found empty. Then I walked into the lounge expecting to find her snoozing in the enormous sofa pit. But she wasn't there either.

Has she left for work?

But I saw her clothes were strewn across the floor with her phone nestled against her jeans.

"What the—?"

I walked back out into the hall ready to run back upstairs. It was a big house, after all. Had she decided to go exploring?

"Becca!"

A crunch sounded from beneath my slipper, and I looked down to see broken glass glittering across the floor amid a puddle of water.

"Becca?"

Something didn't feel right.

"Becca!"

Instantly, the hackles rose along my spine. This wasn't adding up. No Becca, broken glass, her clothes and phone still lying around. Walking briskly from room to room, I searched for her, growing increasingly confused and concerned with each empty room I entered.

"Becca? If you're playing around you can quit now."

But I knew she wasn't fooling around.

This felt wrong.

Call it intuition, or a hunch, but there was a squeezing sensation in my stomach, and it was telling me she was in danger.

When I had checked every room in the house, including the garage, pool, and gym, a sense of dread filled my gut.

The security room, I thought. *That will give me an answer.*

Situated in the outhouse at the side of the garden, the security room used to house a live-in security guard when Olivia had lived here, but I had always found his presence stifling. It was the cameras that did all the work anyway, not him. So when she left, so did he. I seldom had need to enter the place, but now, I barged in and stared closely at all the screens.

"How the hell do I work these things?" I asked myself as I tried to remember.

Twisting the knobs, I focused on all the main doors of the house. Slowly, I rewound through the footage, hoping to find some image of her, but there was nothing. It was like she'd just vanished.

This doesn't make sense. I've checked every room in the house and she's not in any of them. But she didn't leave. And if she did, she left all her clothes behind.

Not sure what to do next, I reached for my phone and called the only person I could think of. Sandra.

"Christ, it's a bit early, isn't it?"

"Are you in the office yet?" I asked, knowing she often liked to put in some extra early hours.

"Is the Pope Catholic? Yeah, I'm here. Just walked in about two minutes ago."

"Is Becca there?"

"No. Should she be?"

"No, it's just that..."

Fuck, what do I say here?

"It's just that I thought she was coming in early today, but she's not picking up her cellphone. Thought I'd give you a quick buzz."

"Well, she's definitely not here. It's just Jerry half asleep downstairs and little old me."

"Well, call me if Becca shows up, alright?"

"She better turn up. You've got that preliminary meeting with the investors' lawyers today, right?"

Shit! How could I have forgotten about that?

"Yeah, I remember. See you soon."

I hung up confused as hell and worried to high heavens.

Where was she?

Dashing back into the house, I searched the lounge, the kitchen and the bedroom again, half-expecting to return to find her sipping an espresso. But there was no sign of her.

"Becca!"

Nothing but the echo of my voice returning to me. I stood on the stairs for a moment listening to the house hoping I could hear her footsteps. My eyes kept darting back to the broken glass. Something wasn't right about that, and somehow, I felt it was the key to everything.

What do I do? Call the police?

No. Not yet. She's around somewhere. Maybe she's gone home or she's back at Bob's. Yeah, that'll be it, she just skipped out on me. She's probably back home laughing to herself about how she spent the night with me and did a runner in the morning.

But why would she leave her phone and clothes?

There was only one logical thing to do next, but my God did I not want to do it. But, knowing I had to, I reached for my phone, took a deep breath, and dialed Bob's number. He answered on the third ring with a yawn.

"Jesus, it's early," he mumbled. "What's going on?"

"Hey. Is Becca there?"

"No. Why would she be? She should be at her apartment."

"Oh. Okay it's just that..."

Think quick! Try not to sound so suspicious.

"I was expecting her in really early at the office today. We've got a big meeting coming up."

"This early? Wow. Better you than me. I haven't seen her. Or heard from her since yesterday. She's probably on her way. Don't fret."

"Alright. Thanks."

"Catch you for a beer later?"

"Sure."

I hung up even more confused than ever.

Something's happened, my mind was telling me. *You've got to call the cops. But what will you say? A girl half your age you slept with last night bailed out on you and you think that's a crime?* They'd probably just laugh at me.

Then it hit me.

You told her you loved her, you moron. No wonder she ran away.

Moving into the lounge, I took a seat where I had made

love to her the night before. Looking down at her clothes and phone, I felt my confusion rise.

Where the hell is she?

I kept thinking about the smashed glass and tried to fit it into the picture. With my head in my hands, I wracked my brain for answers.

Then it came to me. A name I hated so much it felt like a curse.

Olivia...

Could she have had something to do with this?

She was capable of making threats. But she wouldn't hurt Becca, would she?

CHAPTER 25

BECCA

I woke up with a searing pain in my head and the sensation of icy coldness beneath my body. Opening my eyes, I tried to adjust to a blistering light that burned my eyes. Reaching a hand to my head, I felt hot blood run between my fingers.

"Wake up, Sleeping Beauty," condescending woman's voice hissed.

Dragging myself up to a seated position, I tried to figure out where I was. The smell of dust and damp and a cold draft filtering through my hair were not good clues. Eventually, my eyes began to focus on what was in front of me. A long, open floor covered in boxes, crates, and plastic bags.

"Where the hell am I?" My voice was hoarse, my throat incredibly dry.

It looked like something straight out of a horror movie where someone has to saw their own leg off to survive. Thankfully, there were no saws anywhere near me. There was, however, a length of chain running from my left wrist to a water pipe on the wall. I yanked on it and it replied with a clanking sound.

"Oh, our Sleeping Beauty is angry," the condescending voice spoke again.

Through the haze of my headache, I could just about make out the shape of a woman in the distance. She walked toward me, her heels clicking along the floor. As she approached, her face and hair came into view, and I saw her expression of pure hatred.

"Olivia? What the fuck? You kidnapped me?"

She bristled inside her long, fur coat and took another step forward. "I didn't kidnap you," she clarified. "*He* did."

Thrusting a long red fingernail towards the corner of the warehouse, she pointed to a figure dressed in black. The only thing visible was a long, white nose protruding out from underneath a black woolen hat. He looked like an ogre. A beast that could have ripped me to shreds with his bare hands.

I began to shiver and wrapped my blanket around my body tightly with the one hand I could move freely. Olivia laughed and stepped closer, kneeling in front of me so I could smell her expensive perfume.

"What do you want from me?" I asked. "And what the fuck did you do to my head? I feel like my skull's on fire."

"I'm afraid my boy here got a bit too enthusiastic," she explained, her voice dripping with evil. "I told him nothing more than a slap."

"That wasn't a slap! He knocked me out!"

"It's nothing serious," Olivia scoffed as if my bleeding head were nothing. "You'll be fine once the dizziness subsides."

"You're nuts," I spat at her. "Matthew will find me here eventually. You know that, don't you? What do you even think you'll get from this, huh?"

She gave me a sardonic smile and raised herself to her full

height, enjoying the sensation of towering over me in her heels.

"Are you holding me for ransom, is that it?"

"Hmmmm, maybe."

"You are, aren't you? Let me guess. You didn't get as much as you wanted in the divorce settlement, so you thought you'd pull this fucking insane stunt?"

"You're a bright girl," she trilled. "In another life we could have been friends rather than enemies."

"You're not being serious. You kidnapped me for money?"

"Money makes the world go round, honey. What else did you think all this would be for?" She twirled a strand of hair around her finger and walked around in a circle like she was putting on a little fashion show just for herself.

A thought dawned in my head as I looked at her. "It was you who sent those threats too, wasn't it?"

"Oh, I wouldn't call them threats."

"Then what were they? You said you were going to expose Matthew as a sicko. Why would you do such a thing? You'll ruin his life!"

"I didn't actually say I was going to expose him," she replied, a cruel smile on her face. "I just hinted."

"Same fucking difference."

Olivia stopped strutting and dropped the hair from her hand. Walking slowly over to me, she pulled up a stool from beside the window and took a seat. Crossing her legs, she unbuttoned her coat and made herself comfortable.

"Listen to me," she said. "Believe it or not I actually don't have anything against you. You remind me a little of myself when I was your age. Beautiful, driven, ambitious."

"I'm nothing like you," I informed her stiffly. "And I wouldn't want to be."

"And feisty," she added with a smile. "I like that." Leaning forward, she rested a hand on my wrist. "I have an idea," she said. "One that could benefit us both. I want money, and Matthew has plenty of it. I bet you want your hands on it too. What woman wouldn't?"

I stared at her, hoping the disgust on my face was answer enough.

She moved even closer to me so her lips were next to my ear. "If you join me, we can blackmail him together. Two heads are better than one. Double the trouble, double the money. The police will believe you. Tell them he's been grooming you since you were a little girl."

Horrified, I stared at her, speechless for only a moment before I yelled, "No! I couldn't do that! Besides, there's no evidence because it isn't true. It'll never go to trial."

"It won't go to trial, but he'll settle out of court just to hush the story up. Even if it's not true."

Aghast, I could only stare at her. "You're pure evil," I seethed. "I don't know what he ever saw in you."

I reached out my foot and kicked the edge of her stool with as much strength as I could muster. She toppled backward with terror in her eyes, then she fell onto her back, her legs flailing like an upturned beetle. Her hired hooligan rushed over to help her to her feet.

"Tie the bitch up!" she yelled. "And this time you can do more than slap her."

CHAPTER 26

MATTHEW

I lifted my head from my hands when I heard my phone ring. An unknown number flashed on the screen, and I answered it in a heartbeat.

"Hello Matthew." The voice was like nails scratching down the inside of my skull.

"Olivia. What have you done?"

"Calm down," she laughed. "She's fine. Apart from the nasty cut on her head, she's doing just fine."

"Why? Why would you do this?"

"Why does anyone do anything? For money, obviously."

"But, how could you? I checked all the CCTV footage. Looked over every main door of the house. There was no sign of you or Becca leaving."

"There was no sign of me, obviously. What did you think I did? Clobbered her over the head myself and dragged her out of there?"

She let out a maniacal cackle that was so loud it came out distorted through the phone line.

"Besides, you think I don't remember the layout of the house? You think I don't remember that the patio doors to the back of the kitchen were the only exits that weren't covered by the CCTV because of the conifers?"

She laughed again, and I wished I could reach through the phone and throttle the life out of her.

"I think you'll find my man did a good job of remaining hidden."

"Your man? You mean you've pulled some poor bastard into your orbit?"

"This one will do anything for a fistful of dollar bills. He'd kidnap a girl in a heartbeat. He'd hit her if I asked him too. In fact, he'd enjoy hitting her a little harder. He loves violence, Matthew. It's in his blood. All I have to do is say the word and he'll do anything to her. Anything at all. Things you couldn't dream of."

Fear sliced through me as my imagination went insane with horrific things that might be done to her. "Tell me where she is!"

"Do you really think I'd just tell you where she is? You're not a stupid man, Matthew. Don't make stupid demands."

I was holding the phone so tight it hurt. Inside my bath robe, I was beginning to sweat with anger. "I'm calling the cops."

"Call them and she's dead."

I let the words resonate inside my head for a second. She couldn't really mean that. She was a money hungry bitch, but she wasn't a killer.

"You don't mean that."

"Oh, I mean it. I wouldn't have said it otherwise. Call the police and she's dead. Call her dad and she's dead. Do anything at all other than exactly what I tell you and she'd dead. If you want her back, you'll have to give me what I want."

"And what do you want?"

"Ten million dollars."

At first, I thought she had to be joking. I had ten million dollars, but it wasn't as though I just had that kind of cash lying around ready to hand over.

"You're actually fucking serious, aren't you?"

"Ten million dollars or your little plaything dies. It's as simple as that. You've got twenty-four hours."

A click sounded and the phone went dead. I stared at it for a second.

No. You can't let that bitch win. But you can't let Becca die either. If so much as a hair on her head was harmed, you'd never forgive yourself.

With a hand shaking with rage, I dialed the unfamiliar number. This time, a man's gruff voice answered.

"What?" he said, his voice sounding like sandpaper.

"Tell Olivia she can have the money."

There was a snort of laughter from the mysterious man. "Bring it to Apollo Street," he said. "Don't keep us waiting."

I stood in the bank manager's office and watched the look of surprise come over his face.

"Ten million in cash?" he questioned. "I can't just do that. We don't have that kind of money on hand. We keep a limited stock in case of a robbery."

"Please. It's very important that I make this withdrawal. It's…crucial to my business," I lied, not wanting to tip him off that anything was amiss.

Stress was coursing through my veins. I knew that with each passing minute without the money, Becca was in danger.

As I looked into the manager's eyes, I thought of where she could be. Was she injured? What had they done to her? And more to the point had that brute on the phone hurt her?

It must have been the desperation in my eyes, but I saw the manager hesitate for a second then rise out of his seat.

"I'll be right back," he said, disappearing out the door.

I sat for an unbearable few minutes expecting him to return with the police. I wouldn't even blame him for calling them. Me walking in here asking for ten million dollars in cash was suspicious as hell. But I also thought that if Olivia caught wind of the police's arrival, Becca would be dead in an instant.

Suddenly, I didn't view Olivia as my pain in the ass ex-wife; she was a deranged villain who was capable of anything. She wasn't the brightest woman I'd ever met, but right now she was sure as shit the craziest.

The sound of footsteps came from the hall, and I looked up just as the manager opened the door.

"I made a few calls," he said. "I will have to have a truck brought in from another location. You'll have the cash within the hour."

What did ten million dollars look like? If you were to ask me an hour ago, I would have told you it was a stack of cash as high as a building. It wasn't until it was placed in my hands that I realized just how innocuous it looked. Crammed into two large black cases, the money hung heavily from each of my hands.

How the fuck did my life end up like this? I thought as I stepped out of my car onto Apollo Street.

I didn't know what pissed me off the most, that Becca was in danger, or that Olivia was going to get her hands on my money?

It wasn't even the amount of cash that bothered me, it was the fact that she was winning.

She won't get away with this, I thought as I walked down the street.

Apollo Street was situated in the heart of the docks, a place I didn't even think Olivia would know about let alone enter. I scanned the buildings for any sign of life, but there appeared to be nothing and no one. I noticed a black Mercedes parked out front of an abandoned warehouse. As I approached and noticed a light on in an upstairs room, I realized it wasn't abandoned at all.

Pulling my phone out of my pocket, I dialed her number and waited. It rang out, and I hit redial. I called again but got the same response.

The bitch is playing games.

At last, on the third try she answered.

"Tell me you have the money."

"I have it," I told her. "I'm outside."

She hung up. From inside the building I could hear shuffling and the sound of metal doors slamming open and shut. A minute later, the steel grate that covered the entrance slid up to reveal a dark figure the size of a storm trooper. His face was almost entirely covered, but there was a hint of red cheeks beneath his scarf.

"Hand it over," his muffled voice ordered through his scarf.

"Take me to Becca first."

He paused for a second, staring deep into my eyes as though he was trying his best to threaten me. But I wasn't scared of him. I narrowed me eyes and refused to budge as the grip around the cases tightened. His eyes darted down to them, knowing what they held.

"You got it all?" he asked.

"All ten million."

His eyes widened.

"Just take me to Becca," I said. "Or you won't see a single cent."

He looked into my eyes one last time then nodded. "Come with me," he replied. "This way."

I followed him into the building that smelled like damp and decay. The walls were covered in mold and rust and the floors squelched beneath my feet.

Following him through a labyrinth of empty rooms, we eventually emerged in front of a service elevator, the kind you had to yank a huge metal grill across. My first thought was that it was a death trap.

"I'm not getting in that thing. We'll never get out."

"You want the girl, you get in."

I had no choice but to follow him and watch in horror as he pulled the grill across and locked us in. We rode up the building in silence until we reached the top floor. As soon as the doors clanked open, I caught the scent of Olivia's putrid perfume in the distance. It made me sick.

"This way," the meathead said and waved me through a heavy set of double doors.

As we entered, I became aware of signs of life. There was a heater plugged in, a small table with cups and a coffee machine resting on top along with an ashtray. The sound of someone sniffing caught my ear and I turned.

In the corner of the room sat Olivia. There were spots of blood running down the back of her fur coat, and she was holding a wad of toilet paper to her head.

"Your bitch girlfriend made me bleed," she seethed.

"She should have killed you," I replied, feeling a sense of pride in Becca. At least she wasn't going down without a fight. "Where is she?"

"Show me the money first."

I hurled the two cases at her angrily, and they landed at

her feet with two loud thuds. Suddenly the injury to her head made a miraculous recovery and she forgot all about it.

"It's all there?" she gasped, dropping the toilet paper and falling to her knees to open the nearest case.

"Yeah, all your stinking money. It's there."

She opened the case, and I could see the greed shining in her eyes. She was mesmerized by the sight of the cash, and her mouth dropped open as she joyfully squealed.

"You got the cash," I said. "Do whatever the fuck you want with it. Fill your face with more plastic, top up your liver with champagne, fuck off to the other side of the planet. I don't care. Just show me Becca."

She looked up, disgusted, and slammed the case shut. "Is she really worth it?" she asked. "Is she really worth losing ten million dollars?"

"She's worth more than that. Unlike you."

Olivia grabbed the cases of cash, cradling them closer to her body. In that moment, she truly revealed herself as the callous, cruel bitch she really was. Her face morphed into that of a monster's, and her fingers clutching at the cases resembled beastly claws. She wasn't the attractive woman I used to know. She was barely even human.

"Becca's in there," she said, nodding her head toward a door at the back of the room. "Go get her."

I strode over to it, wasting no time in ripping it open. As I burst into the room, I saw her beside the window tethered to a chair wearing nothing but a blanket. There was a long river of dried blood traveling from her temple.

"Matthew!"

"Becca! Oh, God, Becca!" I ran to her, pulling at the ropes around her wrists and ankles.

"I thought you were never coming," she cried. "I thought I was going to die in here."

CHAPTER 27

BECCA

"Get these fucking ropes off me!" I cried, pulling at them.

Matthew's deft fingers worked at the knots, and the ropes fell to the floor.

"Shhh. It's okay," he assured me, holding me tight. "You're safe now. I'm going to take you home, okay?"

All I could do was cry and fall into his arms. For hours I'd been putting up a fight, been desperate to show I was no one's victim, especially not Olivia's. But now that I was safe and free, the emotion was too much to handle. It came flooding out of my exhausted body until I lay in a heap in his arms.

He saved me...Not just me but the baby too.

"Come on. Let's get the hell out of here."

Wrapping the blanket around me, he lifted me into his arms and carried me from the room. As we exited, I waited to see Olivia's smug face. Without my restraints, I could tear her to pieces, but she was nowhere to be seen. And neither was her lackey. The stool she sat on lay on its side, an empty coffee cup on the ground beside it.

"Looks like they took off," Matthew said. "The fucking cowards."

I held onto him as tightly as my arms would allow as he carried me down through the building until I could see daylight filter in through the main entrance. The sun was shining on the sidewalk and the air was crisp. I breathed it in and felt the cool wind create a wave of goosebumps up my arm. A few yards away, I could see Matthew's car. Just a few more feet and I'd be warm and on my way home.

"Freeze!"

Suddenly there was the noise of running boots, of angry voices, and slamming car doors. The sidewalk was no longer covered in sunshine but flashing blue and red lights.

"Boston Police! Let the girl go!"

"No, you've got it wrong!"

"I said drop the girl!"

As I turned my head, I was aware of guns pointing at us as half a dozen officers ran toward me.

"Let the girl go and we won't shoot!"

"Let her go!"

"Drop her now!"

Matthew had no choice but to unravel his arms from around me and let me fall barefoot onto the snowy sidewalk. But as soon as my feet hit the ground, the nearest officer ran at me and scooped me up in his arms.

"Hey! What's going on? Let me go!"

But he wasn't listening but was intent on bundling me into the back of a waiting car.

"What are you doing?"

"It's okay. You're safe now," he told me as he closed the door over.

As he started the engine, I looked out the window just as two officers descended on Matthew, slapping cuffs on him as they pushed him onto the ground.

"What are you doing to him?" I cried. "He did nothing wrong. He saved me!"

"It's okay," the officer said, speaking to me in the rear-view mirror. "He won't get near you again."

I sat in shock in the interview room wearing an old pair of gray sweatpants and a cardigan that an officer had dragged out of lost and found. I felt ridiculous, but at least I was dressed.

"Here. It's not the best coffee in the world. But it's caffeinated and that's what matters, right?" said the friendly female detective as she took a seat across from me.

She barely looked older than I was, and with a fresh face and scraped back hair, she looked like your typical wholesome girl next door.

"I don't know what I'm doing here," I told her. "I don't understand what's happening."

"We got a call from his ex-wife that you were captured."

"I was!"

"By Matthew Banks."

"No, by her! He was the one who rescued me."

"Wait, what?" She looked down at her notes confused. "Are you sure about that?"

"Pretty freakin' sure."

She continued to scan her notes, the confusion in her eyes growing. "She claims he's been grooming you since you were a child. That he's been having a relationship with you since you were twelve years old."

"Twelve! No! We've been seeing each other for a month, tops."

She frowned. "Okay," she said, grabbing a pen. "You're going to have to tell me everything from the beginning."

And I did, gladly. I told her about the threats, the photos, the emails. I told her about being taken from inside the house in the middle of the night by that bear of a man. I explained all about the ransom, the money Olivia said I could have if I lied. I told her about it all. Even me kicking Olivia off her stool.

I told the whole story in glorious Technicolor until the officer had no choice but to slam her notebook closed and let out a long sigh.

"You should be arresting Olivia. Not Matthew."

She shook her head and slurped on her coffee. "Okay," she said. "You can go, and so can Matthew. But stay close. We'll need you both to testify against Olivia."

She led me from the room, and I shuffled out in my oversized sweatpants feeling hideous but grateful we were both leaving. I watched as the detective knocked on the door of the adjoining room before entering. Sitting at the table was Matthew on one side and a burly male detective on the other. She walked over to him and mumbled in his ear. The shock on his face was obvious. He mumbled something back, the two of them having a hushed argument. Eventually, the man stood up and released the cuffs from Matthew's wrists.

"You can go," he said. "My apologies, Mr. Banks. "

But Matthew wasn't listening, because he was running out of the room toward me.

"I told them everything!" I said against his chest. "You should have heard the things they were accusing you of." I wrapped my arms around him and held him tight until I could feel his heartbeat through his chest. "I want to get out of here," I told him. "I want to go home."

We turned to leave, hand in hand as Matthew bent down to kiss my cheek. "Let's go," he said. "I'm taking you home and I'm never taking my eyes off you."

"You'll take your eyes off her right now!" my father's booming voice yelled. "And your fucking hands too."

We both spun around to see Dad at the end of the hallway. His eyes moved from our faces down to our clenched hands.

"Dad..."

"Get away from him." He stepped between us and pulled my hand away from Matthew's.

"You're not going anywhere but back to my house," he yelled furiously, his face red with anger. "You're not going anywhere near this bastard again, you understand?"

CHAPTER 28

MATTHEW

"Bob, please calm down," I said, but I may as well have been talking to the wall.

"Calm down?" he raged. "You two are all over the news! *This* is how I find out about you two! My best friend and my *daughter*? How could you do this to me?"

He stopped yelling and stood breathing heavily. The look on his face turned from anger to betrayal. "How could you do this to my little girl?"

His right hand was clenched at his side as though he was trying to fight back the urge to punch me. "How could you get her into trouble like this? The news said she'd been kidnapped. That she was held in a warehouse."

"Dad," Becca said softly, reaching out to him. "Matthew saved me. I don't know what would have happened if he hadn't arrived when he did."

He pushed her hand away and took a step back. "Do you know what they're saying about you two? Do you know what the rumors are? How could I have been so blind? How could I not have seen this?"

"Bob, I know what you must be thinking, but I love Becca. I love her more than I've ever loved anyone before."

"Love?" he spat. "Love!"

He lunged at me, but before his body could connect with mine, the female detective burst out of the room and pushed him away.

"Get back!" she ordered.

"I should tear your fucking head off, Matthew! You were supposed to be my friend. My *best* friend. I've known you for years. Decades! And you've done this to my daughter? I trusted you!"

The detective wrestled him away from us.

"Dad! We love each other!" Becca cried. "He never made me do anything I didn't want to. He never hurt me. Not once."

But he wasn't listening and continued to rant and yell, almost frothing at the mouth with anger.

"You need to calm down," the detective said. "If you don't, I'll sit your ass in a cell until you do."

"Dad, listen to her!"

Bob, at last, took a deep breath and relaxed. The detective dropped her hands from his arms and took a step back. "All right?" she asked.

"All right," he said and clapped his hands over his face as he tried to compose himself.

"I understand that you're angry, " I told him. "I get it. But you have to know that I love Becca. And she loves me."

He lowered his hands and looked me dead in the eye. "You really love her?"

"I do. I want to be with her. But without your blessing, I can't be."

Becca took my hand and glanced up at me. "Dad, please. I love him. I have for a long time. Won't you be happy for us?"

But he just shook his head, looking ready to explode. "No.

You both betrayed my trust. Especially you, Matthew. You're fucking dead to me."

And with that, he walked away. We watched him leave knowing that it was all coming to a crashing end.

This wasn't supposed to happen.

This wasn't supposed to be how he found out!

"Bob, don't do this," I called. "Don't walk away. Stay for your daughter. Don't you want her to be happy?"

He stopped in his tracks and turned around. "She was perfectly happy before she started working for you! Before she ended up chained up in a fucking warehouse by your psycho ex-wife."

He stormed toward me, pointing his finger in my face as the detective raced to catch up to him.

"I should beat the ever living shit out of you right here and now!"

"Dad, no!" Becca yelled.

Bob's fist lashed out, and before I could stop her, Becca stepped between us as she tried to push Bob away. But his fist, aiming for face, was blocked by her body, and as a scuffle broke out, it landed just above her abdomen. She yelped as she staggered backward, clutching her ribs.

"Becca!" Bob cried. She doubled over in agony, sucking in air as she struggled to breathe. "Becca talk to me," he said, cradling her. "Tell me you're okay."

"Oh, God it hurts!" she cried.

"I didn't mean to hit you. I never meant to hurt you. You gotta believe me."

"The baby," she gasped, her hands clutching her stomach.

"The baby?" Bob asked, his face blanching as he looked up at me.

"I'm pregnant," she said, forcing herself to stand up straight. Her eyes met Bob's, then mine. "Matthew..." she began, her hands clutching her stomach. "Matthew, I'm having your baby."

The detective who had been trying her best to stay out of the drama as best as she could now leaped into action.

"She's pregnant?" she asked, rushing to Becca's side. "If she's been injured, she needs to go to the hospital right away."

CHAPTER 29

BECCA

Dad stood at the end of the hospital bed with a look of shock and disbelief on his face. He looked as though he'd aged ten years over the last hour.

"The doctor said you're going to be fine," he said. "And so is the baby." His eyes were everywhere in the room but on me. It was as though he couldn't bring himself to see my face.

"Yes, we're both fine. Thank God."

He stood up and sheepishly shuffled over. "I'm so sorry I hurt you," he said, tears in his eyes. "You know I would never have hit you on purpose."

"You shouldn't have taken a swing at Matthew either. He did nothing wrong."

The anger returned to his eyes and his cheeks flushed red.

"Dad, please, can we talk about this? I mean really talk about this without you getting so angry?"

He gave a slight, barely perceptible nod and perched on the edge of the bed. "Why didn't you tell me?" he asked, his eyes staring above my head.

"Why do you think? Because of this. Because we knew you'd go fucking crazy. And you did."

"I just wish you trusted me enough to tell me."

"I do trust you, Dad. But I knew how angry you would get. I knew you wouldn't understand that I'm not your little girl anymore."

He hung his head and looked down into his hands. "How long has it been going on?"

"A little over a month."

He looked slightly relieved. "So the rumors aren't true?"

"No, not at all," I assured him. "He's done nothing but treat me wonderfully. He's been a gentleman, Dad. You've got no reason to be angry with him."

"But he should have known better. You're half his age, for Christ's sake. And he's my best friend. It just feels so wrong."

"But to us it doesn't. I love him, Dad. And he loves me." I looked down to my stomach and couldn't believe the surreal turn the relationship had taken. "And I'm having a baby. His baby. *Your* grandchild."

Dad looked ready to burst into tears as he stared at my stomach.

"I wish you hadn't found out like this."

"Nearly died of a heart attack." He pressed his hands into his eyes and sniffed.

I shuffled down the bed and hugged him tightly. I'd not seen him cry in years. Not since Mom died. And seeing tears in his eyes twanged a nerve inside me until I too bubbled over.

"I just can't believe I'm going to be a grandfather. It's the best Christmas present ever," he cried. "My God, I've never been happier, and your Mom...she would have been delighted but... But it's Matthew's baby. I don't know how I'll ever get over the two of you."

With a deep, quivering breath, he composed himself and wrapped his arm around my shoulder. "You really love him?"

"I do. Dad, I could live a thousand lifetimes and never meet anyone like him. I love him so much."

He swallowed hard and looked me in the eye. "You're happy with him?"

"Couldn't be happier."

There was a shift in his eyes. Like a realization swept over him. Like he was seeing it all in a brand-new light. "Okay," he said, squeezing me tight. "I give you my blessing."

"Oh, Dad!"

I squeezed him even harder until I felt as though my lungs were ready to burst, and only broke away when I heard a knock on the door. Matthew was standing in the doorway with a bouquet of roses in his hand. He looked nervously at Dad, then over to me.

"Come in," my dad said. "I won't bite."

Matthew gingerly stepped into the room holding the roses like a shield. "Are you okay?" he asked me.

"The doctor said we're fine."

He stepped in closer and set the flowers down beside the bed. "You're pregnant," he said softy, more to himself than to me. "Why didn't you tell me?"

"I wanted to. Meant to. Kept trying to. But each time I tried, I just couldn't get the words out."

Pulling a chair up beside the bed, he sat down and took my hands in his. "Becca, I promise you I will take care of this baby. I will give him or her everything I have. That baby will never want for anything. The best life possible. And so will you."

Dad looked as though he was ready to tear up again but managed to control himself to reach a hand out and lay it on Matthew's shoulder. "You'll be a great father," he said. "I know you will."

Matthew's face lit up at hearing this, his smile so wide it

illuminated the whole room. "Bob, can we ever move past this? Can we make it work?"

"You're my best friend, Matthew. And I suppose if I can't trust you with my daughter, then who could I trust? It's a shock all right. But I love you both. And I'll love my grandchild more than anything."

Dad leaned in to hug us both, and the three of us rested there, arms around each other in a circle. I'd never been happier or felt so complete.

"I love you both," I said, squeezing them tight.

And I thought of the little one beginning to grow inside me.

And I love you too. You're going to have a great life.

EPILOGUE

MATTHEW - TWO YEARS LATER

I stood on stage with the spotlight burning my eyes. In front of me, the crowd was shrouded in the shadows, but I could feel their eyes on me.

In my hands, the Boston Businessman of the Year Award felt heavy. My fingers were trembling and sweaty around it from the excitement.

When I found out I'd been nominated for the award, I'd laughed at first, thinking it was a joke. But then reality set it and I started to get word that not only was I actually nominated but that I had a real chance of winning.

After all the rumors were circulated after the incident with Olivia, I thought my reputation had been shot to bits and that my business would take a nosedive. I was wrong. Sure, the rumors still spread, but they were quickly dispelled by Becca, who was quick to jump down people's throats to silence them or do all she could publicly to speak out. She'd even appeared on a morning television show to speak of her ordeal and to explain how all of Olivia's allegations were lies created in her deluded mind to get more from the divorce settlement.

Soon, the public didn't see me as a predator or some sort of creep who chased and groomed young girls. If anything, I became a victim of Olivia's insane, money hungry plan. And to my delight, Olivia paid for her stunt. The ridiculous scheme to blackmail me, kidnap Becca, and get ten million dollars landed her fifteen years in jail. She could rot in there for all I cared.

Now, Banks Fitness was bigger and better than ever. But it wasn't just me who had created the empire. I had Becca to thank for that too.

"Thank you, everybody," I said, holding the award tightly so I could feel it was real in my hand. "I can't thank you enough for being here and for choosing me as the recipient of this award. Believe me, this has been a shock. But an incredible one. I couldn't be happier."

I took a breath and squinted into the spotlight. In the center of the room, I could just make out Becca's sparkling red dress.

"Of course," I continued. "It's me up here getting this award. But there's a saying. Behind every great man stands an even greater woman. And that's very much true in this case. I couldn't have built this business to what it is without my wonderful partner, Becca. It was through her vision that Banks Fitness grew to what it is today."

As my eyes adjusted to the lights, I could see her with tears sparkling in her eyes. On her lap, our little girl, Aimee, bounced happily on her knee. She was the noisiest baby I'd ever known, but tonight, she was pleasantly quiet, watching the room full of people with a playful curiosity.

"I'll never forget the day," I said. "The biggest day of my career when I had to meet two investors. Real big shots who would be behind the expansion of Banks Fitness should they choose to dish up the capital we needed. It would have been a big day regardless, but it was just a single day after Becca was so cruelly abducted. And a single day after I discovered I was going to be a father for the first time."

The crowd fell silent, hanging on my every word. People started shifting onto the edge of their seats, eager to hear the rest of my story.

"People told me to not even bother with it. To cancel and take some time to recover. I'd even agreed with them. But do you know who didn't want to take time out? Becca. She wanted to throw herself right into that meeting and wow those investors."

If it was possible, the room fell even quieter as people held their breaths.

"So we pulled ourselves together and walked right into the meeting with the best pitch of our lives. Or rather, Becca did. She did all the talking and gave such an amazing pitch that she simply gave those investors an offer they couldn't refuse. They'd each stood up, shook her hand and said *Thank you very much. Where do we sign?* Six months later Banks Fitness was twice the size it used to be. And today, it's seeing exponential growth in almost every state."

An applause rippled through the room and glasses clinked. From the back of the crowd, I could hear Jake, David, and Bob whoop and yell like the cringey bastards they were.

At the table beside them, Sandra sat with her husband by her side and her own little girl on her knee. She smiled proudly at me like a mother at a school play. I blew her a playful kiss, a sign of my appreciation for her, and she pretended to catch it.

"We've even done something that people said we couldn't do. And not only have we done it well, but we've done it better than everyone else. Banks Fitness now gives a prestige package to younger customers and caters to a more working-class clientele. No longer are we just for the elite. We're for the average guy too. And for that, I also have to thank Becca."

Another wave of applause filled the room, this time louder.

"In fact, what am I even doing standing up here getting this award? It should be hers. Why don't you come on up, honey?"

Everyone turned toward her as she blushed.

"Come on up!" I urged her. "Bring little Aimee too."

With everyone staring at her, she scooped up our little girl and marched onto the stage like the absolute rock star queen that she was. In her arms, Aimee was dressed in a matching red sparkling dress with little booties on her feet. She gurgled and giggled at the crowd, and the crowd melted.

"Ladies and gentlemen, meet the love of my life, Becca, and our beautiful daughter, Aimee."

Everyone clapped at the perfect sight of them. I couldn't take my eyes off my two girls, and in that moment, I was so proud I felt as though I might burst. Filling up with happiness, the joy was too much to control and I found myself tearing up. I swallowed the urge to cry deep inside me. The last thing I wanted was for everyone to see me blubbering on stage.

"So I suppose this is the moment when I hand the mic back and we move onto the next award," I said, looking at the MC in the corner.

He nodded as though willing me to hurry up.

"Except I've got one more thing to say," I said. "Or rather, one more thing to ask."

This had been the moment I'd been planning for weeks, the one that could only happen if I won tonight. I couldn't believe that everything had gone so perfectly that I would now be standing here with my award in one hand, the microphone in the other, and a velvet ring box burning a hole in my pocket.

Setting down the award, I took a deep breath and said, "Receiving this award has been one of the happiest days of my life. But there's one thing that would make it even better."

Becca gave me a quizzical look as if to say *Oh God. What are you going to do now?*

With everyone's eyes still on us, I swallowed my nerves and felt as though my stomach was going to explode with butterflies. With my eyes on hers, I held her gaze and slowly lowered myself to one knee.

"Matthew? What are you...Oh, my God!"

Pulling the ring box from my pocket, I flipped it open and held it up for her. Before I could even get the question out, the room was filled with a deafening roar as people cheered.

"Will you marry me?" I asked, speaking loudly over the tumultuous crowd. I needed to see was the look on her face.

"Yes!" I saw her mouth, and the cheering reached a crescendo. "Yes! Yes! Yes!"

Bowing before her, I slipped the ring on her finger and looked into her eyes, the halo of light from the chandelier shining around her head like a golden crown.

"You've made me the happiest man alive," I told her.

"Oh, Matthew I love you," she said with tears in her eyes. "I love you so much."

The End

Printed in Great Britain
by Amazon